TO CONDEMN THEM

DI SAM COBBS

BOOK FIVE

M A COMLEY

Thank you to the amazing Clive Rowlandson for allowing me to use one of his fantastic photos for the cover.

Happy fell-walking with Alpha and Jet. xx

ALSO BY M A COMLEY

ACKNOWLEDGMENTS

Special thanks as always go to @studioenp for their superb cover design expertise.

My heartfelt thanks go to my wonderful editor Emmy, and my proofreaders Joseph and Barbara for spotting all the lingering nits.

Thank you also to my amazing ARC Group who help to keep me sane during this process.

To Mary, gone, but never forgotten. I hope you found the peace you were searching for my dear friend. I miss you each and every day.

PROLOGUE

"*T*his has to be my dream weekend with my perfect partner. Have I told you lately, James, how much I appreciate you being in my life?"

A smirk appeared, and James glanced at the sky. "Hmm... let me consider that for a moment. Er, the answer would be no, and I think my ego has been suffering lately because of it."

She slapped him playfully. "You cheeky bugger. Anyway, just because I love and adore you, you're still in my bad books for not hitching a ride for hours. My feet feel like they belong to someone else. They're swollen, and I think I have multiple blisters on my blisters."

James threw an arm around her shoulder. "I don't think it's that far now. I'm sorry I've let you down; you have to admit, this is a rarity, I don't usually."

"I know. I'm not really complaining, I promise. Just ignore me."

"That's impossible. Your sparkling wit and spectacular personality are the two things that keep me going most in this dreary life of ours. Let's face it, what is there to look forward to at the moment with the state the economy is in?"

Lorna hugged him back. "Enough, we said this was going to be an economy-whinge-free weekend. Up until now, we've achieved our aim."

"You're right, sorry. I suppose the fact I've failed to hitch a ride is beginning to get to me. Come on, let's shake off the blues and plough on."

They shook out their arms and legs, and Lorna pushed the pain in the soles of her feet aside to endure their journey once again.

"Remind me why I decided to leave the car on the outskirts of Keswick?" James said.

She shrugged. "Pass. It's still a mystery to me."

They continued their walk, and the traffic persisted to whizz past them—that was, until a van eventually drew up slightly ahead of them. Lorna got excited and upped her pace a touch, striding through the pain threshold she'd been complaining about.

James gripped her forearm to restrain her and reduce her excitement. "Wait, we've experienced this before. Some people get off on toying with hitchhikers. They pull over to tease us, and as soon as we get near, they put their foot down and take off again. It's better if we don't show the driver we're too keen."

Lorna heaved out a sigh. She knew he was right, but her feet were suffering from swelling-to-double-the-size syndrome and were in the process of crippling her, making it difficult for her to think straight. "Okay, I hear you. He's cut the engine, which makes me think his intentions are good, unlike any of the others we've come across."

James smiled, and they made their way towards the van at a normal walking pace.

He pulled open the door. "Hi, thanks for stopping."

Lorna peered over his shoulder and smiled. "You'll never know how grateful we are that you've stopped for us."

"No thanks needed. I'll hop out and help you load your rucksacks in the back. It's getting kind of late. We couldn't leave you out here by yourselves, not in the dark. I'm Vic, and this is April." He thumbed over his right shoulder at a pretty blonde woman reading a gossip magazine in the back seat.

Lorna and James smiled and waved.

"Hi, pleased to meet you," Lorna said, her voice cheerfully suppressing the exhaustion tearing at her muscles.

"Likewise," the woman replied. "Why don't you hop in beside me? The men can sit at the front."

Lorna wriggled out of her rucksack, and James took it from her.

"Go on, get in," he said. "We won't be long."

Relieved, Lorna didn't need telling twice. She opened the rear door and climbed in beside April. "We're so thankful you stopped. Not many people seem to stop these days."

"Maybe the pandemic has made drivers more wary of having strangers in their cars."

Lorna gasped. "Damn, I should have considered that. Would you prefer it if we masked up? We've got them in our bags."

"No, don't bother, we're fully jabbed. Are you?"

"Oh, yes, definitely. I was classed as vulnerable during the pandemic. I'm so glad things are more or less back to normal now, although I still tend to wear my mask in the shops. I suppose it has become a habit. Better to be safe, right?"

"Absolutely. You can't be too careful nowadays. The pandemic has changed a lot about how we live our lives, hasn't it? I'm glad we've come through it and are out the other side."

"Yes, it's such a relief. Did you catch it?"

"No. Vic and I both managed to stay clear, which was a miracle in itself. I work in a shop, and Vic is a plumber, so we deal with the public daily."

"Ah right, you were both at the coalface then, when the pandemic was at its worst."

"We were. I felt the public was awful, just horrible to deal with most days. People weren't willing to accept things as they stood and get on with it. I took so much abuse, especially from the older generation, the ones set in their ways." April dismissed her statement with a swipe of her hand. "Anyway, all that is over and done with now. I hope. Onwards and upwards, right?"

Lorna smiled. "Correct. This weekend has been all about that for us. Getting back to nature, enjoying our surroundings more, without the added stresses of everyday life to contend with."

"What jobs do you have?"

"I'm Lorna by the way. I'm a PA, and James is an accountant."

"How exciting. You two make such a cute couple. How long have you been...?" April reached for Lorna's hand and checked her ring finger. "Going out?"

"Gosh, I think it's around three years. Thereabouts, anyway. I'm not one of these women who lead their lives by what's written in a diary."

April laughed. "I'm with you on that one, sister."

The two front doors opened, and James and Vic jumped in.

James twisted in his seat and asked, "Everything all right back there?"

Lorna nodded and smiled. "We're just getting acquainted."

"I bet you could both do with a hot drink, eh?" April raised a flask in her right hand and dug into the bag beside her for two plastic cups. "They're clean, I promise."

4

"That would be wonderful. Is it coffee?" Lorna asked.

"We don't do tea around here. It's either coffee or water."

"Coffee is fine for both of us," James replied.

Vic started the engine and indicated out of the lay-by. "I forgot to ask where you're heading."

"Sorry, I should have checked with you first. Our car is parked in Keswick, is that out of your way?"

"Nope, we're going right past the door, so all is good, mate."

The conversation between the two couples continued, and Lorna felt they built up a great friendship within the thirty-minute drive. The tiredness hit her as soon as she finished her drink. She hadn't realised how shattered she truly was until they had sat down and relaxed. Her head lolled to the side. She stopped talking, and her eyelids drooped. She leaned her head against the window and drifted off into that state between wakefulness and sleep. In the background, the others continued their conversation until she felt the van draw to a halt.

She raised her head. The task drained her of the strength she had left. April was tugging at her arms and wrapping something around them.

"What... what are... you doing?"

Whack!

April slapped her across the face. Lorna's head snapped first one way and then the other.

"Shut the fuck up, bitch!"

Confused, Lorna tried to battle through her lethargy to find out what was going on. Why this woman had abruptly turned on her.

"What the fuck?" James said after receiving what sounded like a thump.

"The less you say the better from now on, you got that?" Vic snarled.

5

Neither James nor Lorna spoke.

Vic jabbed James in the stomach. "I said, have you got that?"

"Yes," James mumbled.

April bent the little finger on Lorna's right hand. "What about you?"

Lorna cried out. "Yes. Why are you doing this?" she dared to ask.

April bent her other small finger back. "No more questions."

"Get her phone off her," Vic instructed.

"Where is it?" April demanded.

"In my rucksack, in the pocket," Lorna replied, her tongue swelling up, at least, that's how it felt.

"And yours?" Vic shouted at James.

"In my jeans."

"Get it."

James withdrew his phone from his back pocket and threw it at Vic then opened the van door and attempted to run.

"Do that and we'll kill her. The choice, as they say, is yours, pal." Vic let out a dark, sinister laugh.

The van door slammed shut again, and James sighed. "Why? What do you want?"

"Questions, questions. What did I tell you about talking?"

"I'm sorry. All I want to know is what you intend doing with us."

"That's for us to know, man. Now give me the keys to your car." Vic pointed at the BMW alongside them.

Reluctantly, James handed over the key fob for his prized possession. "What are you going to do with it?"

"You'll soon find out." Vic hopped out of the van.

James peered into the back seat, and Lorna teared up. "Are you okay?"

"I don't know. My head is fuzzy."

"Mine is, too. You've drugged us, haven't you?" James glared at April.

April smiled. "You were told to keep your mouth shut." She dug her long painted nails into Lorna's hand, drawing blood.

Lorna yelled out.

"Shut your mouth or I'll do something really bad to you."

James turned in his seat. "Please, don't hurt her. She's not well."

"Don't, James. I'm all right."

"You're not," he argued.

"What's wrong with her?" April demanded.

"She has diabetes."

"Is that what you meant by being classed as vulnerable during the pandemic?"

Lorna nodded, and tears dripped onto her flushed cheeks. She really wasn't feeling well.

"Let her go," James said. "Take me as hostage if you need to, just let her go. She won't be able to handle this, I will."

April finished tying Lorna's wrists together and then reached through the front seats to tie James's hands. "No more talking, I mean it, you don't want to mess with us. We've been at this a long time and we know what we're doing. The wise thing to do is not to treat us like idiots, have you got that?"

The van fell silent, and Lorna and James watched on as Vic threw their phones in the front seats of the BMW and then strode to the back of the van. The car park had a few empty cars dotted around, but basically, James and Lorna were alone with these people. Vic returned to the BMW and proceeded to pour petrol over the roof and the bonnet.

"Shit, stop him. That car is new, it cost me a bloody fortune. It's taken me years to save up to buy it."

April giggled. "There's no stopping Vic once an idea starts to fester in that warped mind of his."

"Jesus, what the fuck did we do, to deserve you treating us like this?" James said, his speech slurring.

"Shut up or I'll hurt her again," April sneered. Her gaze was drawn to her accomplice, and a smile tugged at her pink lips.

Struggling to keep her emotions in check, fearing the unknown, Lorna sobbed as she wondered what was to become of them.

"It's going to be okay, Lorna, stay calm, love."

James tried to pacify her, but a feeling of doom swept through her as the first sparks of fire appeared beside them.

Vic jumped back into the van, started up the engine and reversed at speed just in time. The car exploded behind them.

"Jesus. What the fuck is wrong with you? You could have sold it. Why torch the frigging thing?"

Vic laughed, and the van roared out of the car park. April sniggered in the back seat. James peered over his shoulder at Lorna who, by now, was beside herself.

"I'm so sorry," she mouthed at him.

James turned to face the road again and shook his head over and over.

Lorna found everything too much. She finally succumbed to her exhaustion and fell asleep.

* * *

"Right, you wake the girl up, and I'll get him inside."

April did as Vic instructed. She slapped Lorna around the face. "Wakey-wakey, sleeping beauty. It's time to make a move."

Lorna opened her eyes and stared at April.

"Don't give us any shit and you'll be all right, you hear me?"

Lorna nodded. "I don't want any trouble. Where are we?"

April chuckled. "Your home for the foreseeable future. Now get out."

Vic dragged the zonked-out James from the passenger seat and flung his arm around his waist to hold him upright. He opened the front door of the cottage and eased James through the gap and up the stairs to a bedroom. The room was sparsely furnished: a double bed with a bare mattress, a stained quilt with no cover and a couple of equally stained pillows. Vic threw James on the bed and checked his hands were still securely bound, then he went back down the stairs to help April bring the girl into the cottage.

He opened the back door and pulled the slim young woman from her seat.

"Please don't hurt me," she whimpered.

"Shut the fuck up! That's your last warning." He hoisted her onto his shoulder.

She grunted, and then he carried her inside and up the stairs. He threw her onto the mattress; she landed half on the bed and half on top of James.

"Get some rest. We'll be back to check on you in a while."

He left the room and locked the door then put the key, which was attached to a length of string, around his neck and went in search of April. She had lugged their rucksacks into the kitchen. He picked her up and spun her around. "We did it... again."

"I know. I can't believe how gullible these hikers are. What is wrong with them?"

"Yeah, right. Would you get in a van with the likes of you and me inside it? I know I wouldn't."

9

"Desperation always works in our favour, doesn't it?"

"So true. Did you see his face when his fancy car went up in smoke? That has to be the highlight of my week."

April hugged him. "It made me chuckle. Can I ask why you did it? Why didn't you sell it like he suggested? It's got to be worth thirty grand or more."

He shrugged. "Not sure. Apart from disposing of the evidence. I put their mobiles inside, so there's no chance of anyone tracking us back to the cottage."

April ran a hand around his face. "You're amazing. Always thinking on your feet and outside the box."

He smiled down at her. "Teamwork—we're the best team around. If you hadn't drugged them, none of this would have been possible. All this exertion has made me ravenous. How about you knock us up some dinner? Is there anything left in the fridge?"

"Will bacon, sausage, eggs and beans do you?"

"Any chips available?"

"I'm not sure. I'll check the freezer. What about them? Should I cook something for them as well?"

"Nah, let them starve. The drugs will suppress their appetite and should knock them out for the rest of the night."

"She's got diabetes. She should have regular meals, as far as I know. Not that I know much about it."

"She'll be fine. You worry too much. Just be concerned about me and let me worry about them when the time comes." He turned her around, shoved her gently away from him and slapped her backside. "I'm starving. Get me some food, wench."

April giggled and got to work. Within fifteen minutes, she had cooked their feast and laid the kitchen table.

"This is all very civilised," he said. "It smells delicious. You always look after me well. I'll repay the compliment when we go to bed."

Her cheeks flushed. She continued dishing up the fry-up and set the plate in front of him. "Sorry, it'll have to be without chips this time around."

"Not to worry. There's enough here to feed a marching army."

They tucked into their meals, both ravenous from their mental and physical exertions.

After they had devoured every last morsel on their plates, April asked, "What are we going to do with them?"

"We'll have to see how they behave. I'm waiting on a call. We might have to get some money out of them in the mean-time; maybe I should have reconsidered burning the car. It would have been a major problem getting rid of the darn thing. It ain't easy, not without arousing suspicion."

"But the money would have come in handy. Are we going to keep them doped?"

"Yeah, I believe that's the way to go, for now, until we receive the call."

April inclined her head. "Same as the last couple."

"Yep. We did well out of them in the end, right?"

"Yeah, I suppose so."

"Why the sad face?" He held out his hand to her.

"Sorry, I suppose I'm just tired. It's been a long day. I'm ready for my bed. I'll just wash the dishes first."

"There's no need. I'll do that. You go upstairs and get ready for bed. On second thoughts, I'd better sort out some scraps for them and take them up some water."

"I can help."

"Nope, you go up. I won't be long."

They shared a kiss and a little hug, and then April left the room. He tidied up the kitchen then buttered a couple of slices of bread which he threw on a side plate and filled two glasses with water. He placed the items on a tray and carried it upstairs and opened the door. He found the couple still in the same positions he'd left them half an hour before.

He stared down at them, wondering if they were going to be trouble.

Not for now, that's for sure. Sleep well, my angels.

CHAPTER 1

*S*am stretched and jumped when something wet licked her hand. "Crap, you scared the shit out of me, Sonny." Four paws landed on her as her cockapoo rolled towards her for a morning cuddle. She stroked him, and he let out a satisfied moan. Sam turned to look at the clock on the bedside table and threw back the quilt, covering Sonny. "Time for me to get up, sweet pea." Sonny wrestled with the quilt and bounded across the floor to stand in front of her, his tail wagging profusely. "Don't tell me, you want to go in the garden before I get in the shower, right?"

Completely understanding every word that came out of her mouth, except important orders, Sonny ran downstairs and barked at the bottom when she appeared. She tightened her towelling robe and descended the stairs. "Anyone would think the world revolves around you, monkey. What am I saying? It bloody does, most of the time. Come on, in the garden and take care of your business."

After letting him out, Sam filled the kettle and popped a piece of bread in the toaster. She prepared her mug and searched for the peanut butter in the cupboard, which had somehow got buried at the back behind the cereal container. Sonny trotted in through the back door.

"Wait!"

He froze and stared at her. She rushed forward and grabbed the towel off the shelf. First she dried his left front and back paws and then asked him to turn around. Her clever dog obliged, and she dried his remaining paws, kissed him on the nose and removed a treat from the tin.

"Go on, away with you."

He snuck under the kitchen table and scoffed it down. Sam closed the back door just as her toast popped up. After slathering it in sticky, crunchy peanut butter, she completed her task of making her coffee and then took her breakfast upstairs where she hurriedly crawled back into bed to eat it.

"This is the life, eh? One day, when I win the lottery, I might be able to spend a whole extra hour or two in bed before I have to venture out for the day."

Whilst eating her piece of toast, her mind drifted, going over the wonderful weekend she'd spent with Rhys. It had been their second weekend away together, with the two dogs, of course, since they had started going out together.

He was everything Chris, her estranged husband, wasn't. She cringed and took a sip of coffee to ease the stickiness in her mouth. The less she thought about Chris the better. There were days when she found herself wondering how the hell she'd ended up marrying him. He was the total opposite to her usual type, not that she'd had many other fellas before he had come along. Another cringe, and she finished off her toast and left the rest of her coffee to cool down while she jumped in the hot shower.

Fifteen minutes later, when she emerged from the bathroom she found Sonny lying on her pillow. He lifted his head to check on her and then dropped it again.

She laughed. "You're a spoilt brat by anyone's standards."

Sam collected the clothes she had prepared the evening before and placed them on the bed. She dried her shoulder-length brown hair and pinned the sides at the back of her head with a large slide, studied her reflection, wrinkled her nose and shook her hair loose again. "Down it is then."

Slipping on her navy-blue suit and teaming it with the white short-sleeved blouse she had just treated herself to at the weekend down in Bath, Sam finished off her now cold cup of coffee and went downstairs. It was her neighbour, Doreen's turn to look after Sonny today. That task usually fell to either Doreen or Sam's brother-in-law, who was now at the end of his recuperation period from the torn ligaments he'd damaged during a football match. Although, Vernon was guilty of prolonging his recovery after becoming attached to Sonny over the last few months. Either way, she owed them both a lot for getting her out of a fix and not letting Sonny down. Sam slipped on her trainers, took Sonny for a half an hour walk, fed him a light breakfast upon their return, then gathered his supplies together, ready to drop them off next door.

A few minutes later, Doreen opened the door with her usual cheery smile on her mature face. "And a very good morning to my two favourite people... umm, can I say that?"

"You just have. Why not? I regard him as a human, my equal sometimes. I know I really shouldn't, but..."

"Once they get under your skin, they're hard to shift, aren't they?"

"They are. Are you sure you don't mind having him for the day?"

"Of course. I don't have any appointments this week, so feel free to drop him off. You know how much I appreciate his company—well, when I say I, I mean we. You should see when Sonny and Ginger snuggle up together on the rug in front of the fire. I'll see if I can snap a picture of the happy couple today to show you."

"Amazing, who knew cats and dogs could get on so well together? Anyway, here's his dinner and a few treats. Thanks again, Doreen, I'm grateful to you going above and beyond for us."

"Get away with you. Just give me a call later, tell me if you're going to be late or not, if you would. I'm making a sausage casserole if you fancy a portion."

"Sounds yummy to me. You don't have to, though."

"I know I don't. But I want to. You work exceptionally long hours, Sam, it's always a pleasure to help out when I can."

Sam leaned forward and pecked her golden hearted neighbour on the cheek. "You truly are my guardian angel in disguise."

"Hardly. Now you tell me if you're seeing that new young man of yours, won't you? I won't be disappointed if you turn down one of my dinners anytime."

"I will. See you later." She bent to kiss Sonny on the nose again. "Be good for Auntie Doreen."

He licked her face and then darted inside the house.

WHEN SHE PULLED up outside the station, DS Bob Jones, Sam's partner, was wrestling with his crutch, struggling to stand upright after getting out of his vehicle in the heaving car park.

"Hey, let me give you a hand." She lunged forward, but a stark glare from him made her retreat a couple of paces.

"Don't you dare come near me. I am not, I repeat, I'm not an invalid. I can manage, it's just a bit awkward at times."

"I know. This is me backing off but, here's something you're not going to want to hear: there are times when it's all right to ask or even accept help from others. This is clearly one of those times."

Bob swiftly glanced over his shoulder, obviously to see if there was anyone around before he bowed to her wishes. "All right, just this once. I struggle to get out of the car and up onto the pavement. My momentum, or lack of it, seems to take a toll on my stability."

Sam scanned the area herself and dashed forward to aid him. "Tell me what you need."

"Can you hold me upright while I get my crotch, I mean crutch, in place."

They both ended up in a fit of giggles.

"Even when the world is against you, you can still make me laugh, partner. Don't ever lose that ability or your crass sense of humour, will you?"

He huffed and leaned heavily on the metal crutch. "Charming, that is. I'm trying my hardest not to be too reliant on those around me, believe me."

They hobbled up onto the pavement, and he pressed the key fob to lock his car. "You can get your hands off me now. If anyone were to come out of the station and see us this close, they'd think you were taking advantage and groping an invalid."

She laughed again. "Wishful thinking on your part. I'm fussy about the men I touch up, thanks all the same."

"Kick a man when he's down, why don't you?"

Sam strode ahead and opened the main door for him and then used her security card to get through the inner one. "We'd better take the lift. Has the hospital said how long you're going to be incapacitated?"

They hopped into the lift, and Bob fell against the glass wall at the rear. "Another week should see the bone mended, and then there will be a certain amount of physio to suffer through, I suppose. I'm not really sure, I kind of switched off when they told me it would be six to eight weeks in a cast. You don't realise how debilitating it is until you have one strapped to your leg. A dumbbell would have been less of a struggle to deal with, I can tell you."

Sam's sympathy gene prodded her. "I've never been in that situation, so I wouldn't know. And I definitely wouldn't have stood in the way of a speeding van in the first place."

She turned away from him, suppressing a giggle, aware of what would come out of his mouth next.

"Bloody hell, how many times are you going to remind me of that faux pas?"

"Once or twice more should do it. Do you think you'll listen the next time you find yourself in a similar position?"

"I doubt it. It was a spur-of-the-moment thing, you'd have done the same, don't go telling me otherwise."

"Who knows how anyone is likely to react in such a grave set of circumstances? Anyway, let's move on. We've got the paperwork to finish up on the last case we solved. I'm sensing the lull we've just been through this past week is about to change soon."

"Copper's instinct or women's intuition telling you that?"

"Is there a difference?" She grinned.

After the lift juddered to a halt, they took the slow walk along the corridor to the incident room, where they were cheerfully greeted by the rest of the team. Sam carried out the honours of making coffee for herself and her partner then went through to her office. She attended to the usual dross that kept her tied to her desk for a good couple of hours at the start of every day, if she allowed it, and was just about to rejoin her team when the phone rang.

"DI Sam Cobbs, how may I help you?"

"Sorry to trouble you, ma'am, it's Nick on reception. I have a lady here who is looking for a bit of guidance and I wondered if you wouldn't mind coming down and having a brief chat with her."

"About what, Nick?"

"Her daughter has gone missing."

"I see. Ordinarily, as you know, that's not usually something we tend to deal with, Nick."

He sighed and lowered his voice. Sam imagined him turning his back on the woman behind the reception desk so she couldn't hear what he was saying.

"She's pretty distraught, has reason to be fearful for her daughter's life. I wouldn't be ringing you if I felt you weren't up to dealing with it, if you get what I mean, ma'am."

"I do. All right, give me five minutes to finish off this paperwork and I'll be down. Do you want to show her through to an interview room?"

"I'll do that and ask her if she wants a drink while she waits."

"Good. Good." Sam ended the call, tidied up a few papers and left her seat. She took in the sight of the hills in the distance, inhaled a steadying breath and left her office. "I won't be long. There's someone downstairs wanting a chat with me."

Bob frowned and attempted to get to his feet. "Want me to come with you?"

"No, you stay here. It's probably something and nothing."

"Is it personal? Anything to do with that shit of a husband of yours?"

"No, it's to do with work. I wouldn't let anything personal come before work, you should know that by now, partner."

"Yeah, I did think twice before mentioning it."

"I'll be back before you know it."

She left the incident room and worked her way down the concrete stairs to the reception area. "Where is she, Nick?"

"I've put her in Interview Room One, ma'am, with a nice cup of tea. Just to warn you, she's a bit shaken up."

"You mean emotional, right?"

He nodded.

"I'll bear that in mind. What's the lady's name?"

"Mrs Vanessa Farrar."

Sam smiled and marched along the narrow corridor to the interview room at the end. She opened the door and entered to find a blonde woman, in her late forties to early fifties, sitting at the table. A designer Gucci bag beside her, matching the smart suit she was wearing.

"Hello, Mrs Farrar. I'm DI Sam Cobbs."

When she glanced up, pain swam in her eyes. "Oh, hello. Please, call me Vanessa."

"Very well." Sam pulled out the chair opposite her and slapped her notebook on the table. Settling into her seat, she flipped open the pad and poised her pen. "Why don't you tell me why you're here today?"

Vanessa inhaled a large breath and closed her eyes. "My daughter and her boyfriend went missing on Sunday. I've been frantic, going out of my mind with worry ever since."

"I see. Do you know their whereabouts when they went missing?"

"Yes, they always leave the car at Keswick and hitch a ride farther into the national park. They climb the fells, they like to challenge themselves, choose a different walk every time they go up there."

"Any specific reason as to why they leave the car at Keswick?"

"I think just so they can get a proper feel for the experience. And yes, I'm always alerting them to the dangers of hitchhiking, but they're young and stubborn in their thoughts, they know best... except when they don't."

Sam nodded. "Sounds about right. What age is your daughter?"

"Lorna is twenty-three, and James is twenty-four, I believe."

Sam jotted down the information. "Sorry, James's surname is?"

"Campbell. I apologise, I should have said."

"No need for that. Obvious question, presuming they both have mobile phones, have you tried contacting them?"

Vanessa sniffled and dipped her hand inside her handbag to extract a pretty lace hanky. She wiped her nose. "Yes. Nothing. There's something else. My husband and I went looking for them yesterday and found James's car burnt out in a car park."

Sam glanced up from her notebook and frowned. "Are the local police aware?"

"Yes, there was a police car at the scene. The fire brigade had been called out to tackle the blaze the night before, on Sunday."

Sam sucked in a breath and let it out slowly. "I have to ask, could either Lorna or James have been inside the vehicle when it went up in flames?"

"No. I asked that same question and I was reassured that there were no bodies inside the vehicle. That's the part that doesn't make sense to me. Their car goes up in smoke, and they are nowhere to be seen."

"And what did the officer at the scene have to say?"

"Not a lot in all honesty. I had to restrain myself. Surely, he could recognise these weren't normal circumstances. Well, a car doesn't just burst into flames by itself while it's parked up somewhere, does it?"

"You have a point. I'll try and get my hands on the report after we conclude our meeting. Did the officer mention if the Scenes of Crime Officers had attended the scene?"

"They were due to turn up any moment. My head was spinning. My husband felt it was better for us to leave them to it and go home. I haven't been able to sleep or rest properly, knowing that they're both out there somewhere, hurt for all we know. I just want some answers, Inspector."

"I'd feel the same in your shoes. Let me try and chase up the report now before we go any further. Can I get you another drink while I'm out there?"

"Thank you, that would be very kind of you."

Sam left the room, trotted up the corridor and ran up the stairs to the incident room. She made a beeline for Sergeant Claire Owen, their resident computer expert. "Claire, I need you to do me a favour."

"I'm all ears, boss."

"I need you to chase up a report for me. A car was found in a Keswick car park, burnt out on Sunday."

Claire's fingers flew across the keyboard, and seconds later, she pointed at her screen.

Sam shifted position to peer over her shoulder. "Damn, I was hoping we'd have more than that on the incident. All it says is the officer thought an accelerant had been used."

"It's probably too soon, boss. SOCO need to do their thing, that's usually when information begins to get gathered, but you know that."

Sam puffed out her cheeks. "Don't I just? Okay, it was worth a punt. Thanks for checking, Claire."

She started back towards the exit, but Bob clutched her arm. "Hey, slow down, you're going to cause yourself a heart attack. What's going on?"

"Two missing people and one burnt-out vehicle. It's not looking good to me, partner. I'd better get back to her. The mother of the girl is in a bit of a state, which is understandable."

"Want me to come with you?"

"No, I'll be fine. Gotta fly." With that, she pushed through the door and raced back down the stairs, stopping off at the reception area to grab Vanessa another cup of tea and a coffee for herself.

"How's it going?" Nick asked tentatively, handing her the cups.

"You were right to call me. There's more to this case than simply two missing persons."

Nick nodded. "I had a feeling you might say that. Anything I can do?"

"Not really. Except keep us topped up with drinks."

"You've got it. I'll drop by in half an hour or so."

"I appreciate it, thanks, Nick. Right, I'd better get back in there, she'll be wondering where I've got to."

"Good luck."

Sam hurried along the corridor, and once she'd entered the room, deposited the cups on the table. "Sorry for the delay. I had a wasted trip. We won't know more about the incident until SOCO have given us their report. All we know thus far is it was likely an accelerant started the fire."

Vanessa sighed and stared at her cup. "That's what my husband thought. He could smell the petrol at the scene, but the officer we spoke to refused to comment."

"Maybe you can fill me in on your daughter and her boyfriend's relationship. Do they get on well together?"

"Oh yes. James is a real gem. Treats her like a princess. The best boyfriend we could hope for her to meet, from a parent's point of view. Very attentive. They rarely, if ever, argue. He thinks the absolute world of her, and she of him. A match made in Heaven my old gran would have said, had she ever met him."

"He sounds wonderful. How long have they been going out?" Sam flicked to another clean page in her notebook.

"Three years."

"And what do James and Lorna do for a living?"

"James is an accomplished accountant in his uncle's firm, and Lorna is a personal assistant to a man running several successful companies."

"I'll need their particulars."

"Yes, I can look those up for you on my phone." She did and issued Sam with the information.

"I have to ask if either of them has mentioned anything untoward going on at work lately."

"No, nothing that comes to mind. They both love their jobs, never thought about ditching them and going somewhere else, if that's going to be your next question."

"It was. Do you know if either of them is in any kind of financial trouble?"

"No. They're very good with money. They're not like other youngsters their age, they've been saving hard to buy a house, which is a feat in itself these days, with the price of houses skyrocketing every year. My husband and I have told them that if they save a substantial amount for a deposit, we'll match it."

"That's a kind gesture."

"It's what families do for their loved ones, isn't it?"

"You'd be surprised. Not all families find themselves in such a privileged position."

"Ah, yes. I suppose you're right. My husband is a solicitor with his own firm. He's been super successful over the years, and we've been quite frugal with our money, unlike some of our friends."

Sam raised an eyebrow and glanced down at the woman's handbag.

"Ah, okay, you've caught me out. All right, we do spend a little of our money on extravagant things. Anyway, getting back to Lorna and James, my biggest concern is the fact that my daughter has diabetes."

"And she takes regular insulin?"

"Yes. She would have taken the insulin with her, but I'm not sure if she would have taken enough with her to have lasted this long, that's why I'm so worried. My husband thinks I'm being daft, worrying like this, but I suppose that's where a mother's instinct kicks in, and something doesn't feel right about the way they've just disappeared, and it doesn't explain what happened to James's car either."

"Are you telling me you're a close family?"

"Very close. If they were in any form of trouble, Lorna would have called us straight away. But what if she's unable to? What if someone has abducted them?"

Sam raised a hand to reassure the woman. "Let's not run before we can walk here. There could be any number of reasons why your daughter hasn't got in touch with you."

Vanessa fidgeted in her seat. "Such as? Please fill me in, because I think I know my daughter better than you, Inspector."

"I didn't mean that to come across as rude. All I'm trying to do is allay your concerns until we have some evidence or possible clues at our disposal. What about their phones?"

"I understand. I apologise for snapping. I've tried ringing them, of course I have. Nothing. You have to believe me, there's no reason for either James or Lorna not to get in touch with us. You're forgetting a vital part of this perplexing puzzle: the car and the fact it was set on fire. It was a new car, less than a year old, and James's pride and joy. There is no way he would stand back and allow someone to set fire to it without putting up some kind of fight to prevent it."

Sam noted down the woman's concerns. "Okay. The main issue that is troubling me is that you haven't been able to make contact with either of them. So we have two young people missing, their car torched, and you're unable to make contact via their mobiles."

"I'm glad we're on the same page, Inspector, plus you're going to need to consider that my daughter is vulnerable, a diabetic. Without her insulin…" She shook her head. "I don't even want to contemplate the consequences."

"I'm sure. When was the last time you spoke to your daughter? Can I have their phone numbers, to make some checks?"

"Oh yes, let me see." Sam jotted down the numbers she gave her. "Now where was I? Oh yes, on Sunday. She was very excited about the adventure. They were all prepared. James is a seasoned walker, his family have been crossing the fells for years."

"So he knows his way around up there."

"Yes. My first thought was that they had reached the summit and they'd had an accident, but then my mind keeps going back to the car."

Sam nodded. "Yes, so does mine." *I'm doing my best not to go down that route, but it does sound like something drastic has happened to this couple. What, though?* "Were they setting off on this adventure alone?"

"Yes. Although they usually venture up there in a group. This time they decided to go by themselves."

"Do you know why?"

"Because they've both been working really long hours lately and said they preferred to spend some quality time together. Also, Lorna has had a rough couple of months with her diabetes. She's been stable for the last few weeks, well enough to take off on a hike. I did try my best to dissuade her, but it was pointless, she wouldn't listen. I'm not a believer as such, but maybe I had a premonition that something would go wrong." A lone tear slid onto her cheek, and she swiped it away. "Sorry, I swore I wasn't going to break down and cry. I know it doesn't get you anywhere in this life to show your vulnerability."

Sam patted Vanessa's hand. "Your secret is safe with me. This is a very difficult situation for you to deal with, you're allowed to show your emotions. I'm not here to judge you for being a compassionate human being."

"Thank you. It's not the done thing amongst my circle of friends. We must present a stiff upper lip at all times, we have to, otherwise people won't take us seriously."

"Like I said, there's no need for you not to lower your guard in front of me."

"You're very kind. I like you, Inspector. I've had the misfortune of dealing with several officers in the past, at functions I've attended with my husband, and I can honestly say I've never met someone as caring as you."

Sam's cheeks heated under the woman's gaze. "I have my moments, I assure you. But I'm aware of what you must be dealing with right now. The gravity of the situation is obvious to me and something I'm going to relish taking on."

"Thank you, that's a relief to hear. I'm not overexaggerating the need to find them, especially with my daughter's condition."

"Don't worry, my team and I will begin the investigation as soon as this interview is over."

"How? Where will you start?"

Sam chewed the inside of her mouth. "We'll begin by tracing their phones, or trying to locate them and go from there."

"What about going to the press, using the media to locate them? Is that even possible?"

"We'll do what we can from this end first and then call on the press if all else fails."

"I see. Maybe putting their photos out there could be beneficial from the start, rather than leaving it a few days to see what arises. Not that I'm trying to tell you how to do your job at all."

"It's fine. You're going to have to trust me. Let's do the relative digging first and then see where we stand regarding the media exposure."

"Of course. I trust you, Inspector. Please, don't let me down. I need my daughter back, she's our only child."

"All I can advise is for you to remain calm throughout the process. I promise we'll do our best to bring Lorna and James home to you all. May I ask what aroused your suspicion that something was wrong?"

"Lorna told me that she would check in with me once they were on their way home. She failed to do that. My husband insisted we leave it overnight, and that's when we went looking for their car." Her head dropped. "I've never hated my husband as much as I do right now... I'm sorry, that's an awful thing for me to say. There again, if he hadn't insisted on holding off, maybe, just maybe, we might have found them by now."

"I can understand your anxieties, but at times like this, you and your husband are going to have to stick together to get through what lies ahead of you."

"I know. It's much harder than anyone realises once the blame game comes into play."

"I have no doubt about that. What about their friends, have you tried to contact them? Maybe they've heard from Lorna and James."

"I rang her best friend, Deanna, and she hasn't heard from Lorna since the beginning of last weekend, when they went into town together, clothes shopping."

"Do you have her number? What about James's friends, any luck there? Or his family perhaps?"

After Vanessa gave her the friend's number she said, "I'm in touch with his father, he works alongside my husband, they're good friends. That's how James and Lorna met, through their fathers."

"I see. And do you know when James's father last spoke to his son?" *Why hasn't his family reported him missing?*

"On the Sunday, around the same time we spoke to Lorna. He was excited about their adventure. His father has also spent many an hour up on the fells, that's where James's interest in fell-walking came from."

"And James sounded okay? Apart from being excited?"

"As far as I'm aware, yes."

"Do they live together?"

"No, both kids are still at home. Not exactly kids, but they are to us."

"Because of their finances and trying to save for a house together?"

"That's correct. Renting is such a waste of money, don't you agree? They can come and go as they please; James stays over most weekends. This weekend was about spoiling Lorna, and now… this has happened." Vanessa sniffled and wiped her nose once more.

"Try not to get upset, I know that isn't easy. Can you give me your address and James's?"

Vanessa cleared her throat, gave her own address and then scrolled through her contacts in her phone to find James's. "What will happen now?"

"You're going to have to leave this with us for a few days. One last question. Do you have a recent photo of Lorna and James?"

Again, Vanessa picked up her phone and scrolled through the photo section. "How's this, or are they smiling too much in this one? Yes, they are, skip that one. Let me see if I can find a better one."

Sam smiled and agreed with her, the first picture was too smiley for what she intended it for.

"Ah, here we are, they're both looking thoughtful in this one."

29

Vanessa angled her phone towards Sam.

"Yes, that would be perfect. Can you forward it to me?" Sam gave Vanessa her mobile number, and her phone pinged, signifying that the message had arrived. "Excellent, we'll get the image printed off and circulated. Now, is there anything more you can tell me that you think might be relevant to the case?"

"No, I don't think so. Will you circulate the photo right away?"

"To our colleagues, yes. They'll keep an eye open for the couple. Would there be any point in me asking you what Lorna and James might have been wearing on their hike?"

Vanessa winced and chewed her lip. "I'm not sure. Lorna always wears a navy-coloured jacket, but that's through the winter, it's June now, although it can get a little nippy up on the fells. She tends to tuck a waterproof jacket into her backpack for emergencies. Sorry, that wasn't really helpful, all that rambling. The answer is no, unfortunately, my husband and I were attending church when they set off."

"Don't worry. I'll keep you up to date with our progress. I can't promise that I'll get in touch every day, but maybe every other day will suffice?"

"It will." Vanessa crossed her fingers. "I hope you find her, I mean *them*, soon. I'm worried about what will happen to my daughter if she hasn't taken enough insulin with her."

"Try not to think about that, it'll only make you worry all the more."

Sam rose from her chair, and Vanessa followed her to the door.

At the main entrance, Sam gave Vanessa a business card. "Ring me day or night if you hear from either of them."

"Thank you. I will. Thanks again for seeing me so promptly. I'm sorry if I've come across as a clucky mother hen."

"You haven't. Do you have a car here?"

"Oh yes. I never rely on taxis or public transport."

"Take care driving home."

"I will. Good luck, I'll speak to you soon, hopefully when you have some good news to share."

"I'll be in touch, don't worry. Take care of yourself."

"I will."

Sam held the door open and watched Vanessa get in a black Lexus parked on the other side of the car park. She waved as the woman reversed and drew away.

"How did it go?" Nick asked.

Sam heaved out a sigh. "I fear this case is going to be a struggle to get our heads around. Nothing Mrs Farrar has told me is making sense right now."

"I'm sure you'll sort things out soon, ma'am. You always do, especially when your back is against the wall."

"It's definitely going to be that. Must crack on. See you later. I've got a photo of the couple. I'll get some printed off for you to distribute amongst the troops, if that's all right, Nick?"

"I was just about to suggest the same."

Sam ran up the stairs and handed her phone over to Claire to deal with the image while she brought the whiteboard up to date with the information she had gathered from Vanessa, which hadn't really amounted to much, not really.

Claire collected the photos from the printer. "Gosh, I hope they're all right and nothing nasty has happened to them."

"Yeah, I'm hoping the same. They're both from relatively wealthy families. So the lowdown is this, folks. Lorna and James set off on a hike on Sunday morning. We're unsure which fells they decided to walk, but they left their car in Keswick. The car was later found burnt out. Her parents got worried about them and went out the following day, searching the area where they usually leave their car and found the vehicle and a police officer at the scene. You can imagine how upset the mother and their families are finding this. However, there's another reason why she came to see me in person to seek help. Lorna is a diabetic. This weekend was a treat for her as she's been through a slightly rough patch with her condition lately."

"Damn, that's not so good," Claire said, her mouth pulled down at the sides. "My friend has diabetes and has to follow a very strict routine to keep it under control. Do we know if Lorna has extra insulin with her?"

"We don't. Lorna is twenty-three and in charge of her own medication routine. Claire, can you do the necessary research for me, regarding the needs of a diabetic and what the time frame is before we should really start panicking? I know we're in the dark about what backup insulin she has with her but the longer she's missing, I'm taking it, the more we should be worried, right?"

"I'll get the information from my friend and search the internet. I'm by no means an aficionado on the subject and would hate to offer the wrong advice. I do know that my friend failed to take her insulin on time a few years back, missed it by a couple of hours, and she went weird."

"In what way, can you remember?"

"Sorry, I meant she couldn't stop drinking, she was exhausted, had the urge to wee more, was light-headed, maybe a little delusional."

"Okay, isn't there an ultimate fear that a diabetic could fall into a coma?"

Claire sighed and nodded. "I told my friend off for not warning us that could happen. Anyone with diabetes needs to take proper care of themselves. If they're unable to do that, then yes, the likelihood is that Lorna might fall into a coma."

"Shit! I knew it could be serious, no wonder the mother is

going out of her mind with worry. Okay, let's start doing all we can to bring these two young people home again."

"Umm... at the risk of sounding like an idiot," Bob stated, "where do we bloody begin on this one?"

Sam's mouth twitched. "I wish I knew. I suppose we check with friends and family, maybe extend that to include work colleagues, see if anything has happened in their recent past. Other than that, we carry out the background checks on each of them and use their phone numbers to check their last location with the service providers. As time is of the essence, Claire and Suzanna, why don't you team up to do that?"

Suzanna rose from her seat and dragged her chair over to Claire's desk. "Will do, boss."

"And what do you want the rest of us to do?" Bob asked.

Sam paused to think if she'd had a similar investigation they'd been tasked with and how the case had proceeded. She couldn't think of one. "I'm at a loss about what to think right now, Bob. Help me out, anyone?"

The rest of the team looked at each other and shrugged.

"There'd be no point in searching for CCTV, not on the fells. We could search around Keswick, see if we can spot their vehicle and if anyone else was maybe following them," Alex suggested. "Other than that, I don't know."

"Good idea. Why don't you and Liam do that? Let me know if you find anything."

"Bob, if I give you Lorna's best friend's number, can you sensitively ask her some questions?"

"What are you saying? That I usually don't give a shit when I question people?"

"Did I say that? I meant go softly, softly with her. I imagine they're very close, and she'll be worried about her dearest friend."

"Only if you can trust me." He issued a smug grin.

33

Sam pulled a face at him. "I'll be in my office, ringing James's father, see what he has to say." Not that she was looking forward to speaking to him, she had a mental block and broke out in hives whenever she spoke to solicitors lately. What with the imminent divorce and the fact that her husband had been carrying on with one behind her back for months before they had separated. She shuddered at the thought.

"Are you all right?" Bob was quick to pick up on the tension running through her. "Maybe we should swap calls," he suggested.

Sam smiled. "I'll be fine. Shoulders back, must crack on. Let me know if you find out anything."

"Ditto," Bob hollered after her.

She settled into her chair and spent the next few seconds inhaling and exhaling repeatedly until her heart rate had slowed to near normal again. She dialled the number and asked to speak to Patrick Campbell.

"Hello, I'm afraid Mr Campbell is on the other line at the moment. Can I pass on a message, or would you like me to get him to ring you back once he's finished?"

"Yes, that would be great." Sam introduced herself and gave the woman her direct number.

"He shouldn't be long."

"Thanks. Goodbye." She ended the call and tackled some emails and letters to while away the minutes before Mr Campbell finally got back to her.

Her phone rang.

"You wanted to speak with me, DI Cobbs?"

"I did, sir. It's regarding the disappearance of your son. Mrs Farrar paid me a visit this morning, and I've agreed to take on the investigation into the missing persons' case."

He fell silent, and then a heavy sigh filled her ear. "I'm as distraught about Lorna and James going missing as

Vanessa and Oscar are. Oscar and I were speaking about it before we started our daily routine. He told me that Vanessa planned on going to the station to report them missing. None of us know what to make of it. This is so unlike our children to behave this way. There has to be something wrong. They're generally in contact with us at all times, and we've heard nothing. They're not answering their phones—that in itself tells me there is something drastically wrong here. We just want to know what is going on and what we can do about it. Sorry, I'll let you get a word in now."

Sam smiled. "I'm here to help, sir. I had a lengthy chat with Vanessa, and she gave me the impression that you're all very close. She also said it was unlike James and Lorna to be out of contact with you all."

"That's correct. Which is why we're so troubled by their disappearance. Factor in that Lorna is diabetic, and you can imagine the stress and worry we're all having to deal with at this time."

"Yes, I'm aware of that. It's a great concern for me, too. I'm hoping my team and I will be able to alleviate some of the stress for you. I wanted to touch base with you, firstly to try and put your mind at ease and also to find out a bit more about your son."

"Okay, what do you need to know?"

"If anything has happened in his life, in the last few months perhaps, that has caused him any kind of concern."

There was a slight delay before Mr Campbell responded. "I can't think of anything. He's a good man. Settled in his job as an accountant at his uncle's firm. I could have a word with Raymond, my brother, see if there have been any problems with any clients lately, if you like?"

"That would be wonderful. Maybe you can get your brother to ring me directly, or I could ring him perhaps?"

Patrick reeled off a number, and Sam jotted it down on a spare piece of paper.

"Thanks, I'll contact him after I've finished speaking with you. What about their friends? Have they fallen out with anyone lately?"

"Not that I'm aware of. Lorna and James are both very easy-going, not the type to fall out with people at the drop of a hat."

"Good to know, it's a help anyway. Do either of them have any siblings?"

"No, neither of them. Not doing very well here, are we? I swear I'm not trying to make your life harder, Inspector. There's just nothing I can think of why two young people, out on an adventurous outing on a Sunday, should go missing."

"We're going to do our very best to find out, sir. When was the last time you had any contact with James?"

"Either Saturday or Sunday, I can't remember which. He told me how excited he was to be going away with Lorna. No doubt Vanessa filled you in about Lorna being off-colour lately?"

"She did."

"Well, this was my son's way of giving Lorna a reward, if you like, for getting better. And now we find ourselves in this situation, both of them missing and his brand-new car torched. That can't be right. It just can't be. There's no reasonable explanation for them to go missing, none."

"Okay, I just wanted to get in touch with you to assure you that we're going to do our best to bring James and Lorna home to you soon. You have my number, please get in touch if you hear from them, or anyone else for that matter."

"Anyone else? Are you saying what I think you're saying? You're expecting us to receive a ransom demand?"

"It's a possibility we have to be prepared for, yes. Not to

put too fine a point on it, James and Lorna are from wealthy families. That has to be an aspect we need to take into consideration, don't you agree?"

"Sadly, I fear you might have just made a fair assumption. If you'll forgive me, one that I'm not willing to accept just yet."

"I don't want to either, but it's an option we need to bear in mind all the same. Goodbye, Mr Campbell."

"Do your best for us, Inspector."

"I will, you have my promise." Sam ended the call and glanced out of the window at the fluffy cumulus clouds floating past. She'd love to climb aboard one and drift around the fells, searching for the two missing people she was now in charge of locating. A knock on the door interrupted her daydream. "Come in."

Bob pushed the door open and hobbled into the room, bashing his crutch on the edge of the door as he passed it. "Damn thing keeps getting in the sodding way. I don't think I'm ever going to get used to it, it's just not coming naturally to me."

"You'll get used to it, and then it'll be whipped away from you. What's up?"

He threw himself into the chair and stretched his leg out beside the desk. "Just wanted to let you know what the friend said."

"And?"

"Nothing much. Except she did mention that she and Lorna had a run-in with a couple of guys at a pub a few weeks back."

Sam inclined her head. "A run-in? How did that manifest itself?"

"They were out for a drink, and the two guys kept pestering them, offering to buy them top-ups, and when they said no, they kept pushing. The two girls ended up moving to another pub, and ten minutes later, the blokes showed up and started coming on to them again."

"No, that sounds horrendous. Blatant harassment. What happened?"

"The girls had a word with the management at the second pub, and the two men were asked to leave. They kicked up a fuss, said they had as much right to be here as anyone. The manager and a couple of the barmen ended up escorting them off the premises."

"Were Lorna and her friend okay after that?"

"Yes, a touch unnerved by the incident, but they got home safely enough. Although, Lorna was a little on edge for a while afterwards."

"Hmm… maybe the problem sparked something going wrong with her condition and led to her feeling unwell."

"Yeah, that's what Deanna put it down to. She's devastated Lorna and James are missing. All she's been thinking about is that incident."

"Did you get the date it happened and the names of the pubs, Bob?"

He grinned. "This is going to shock you. Yes, I did. I've since rung both establishments and asked them for any CCTV footage they might have of the incidents."

Sam smiled. "There, you've earned yourself a cream cake for lunch. See, you are capable of thinking for yourself occasionally."

He closed his eyes and shook his head. His eyes opened again, and he said, "I might have known you'd come out with a comment like that."

"Sorry to be so predictable. Keep on top of the pubs, make sure we get that footage within the next few days."

He tapped the side of his head with the pen he was holding. "Yep, already thought about that. What about you? How did it go with the lad's father?"

"Nothing much to report. He's given me his brother's number, that's where James works, I was just about to give him a call."

He placed his crutch upright beside him and used it to lever himself out of the chair, huffing and puffing through his exertions. "I'll leave you to it then."

"Are you all right? I want to give you a hand but I know you're likely to snap my head off for assisting you."

"Yeah, I'm an independent fucker at the best of times. It won't affect my work, though, boss, you can be sure about that."

"I know, Bob. However, if we get any leads and I need to get out there, I might need to take someone else with me from time to time."

"Granted. I've already considered that being an option. I think I'd be more of a hindrance than a help, especially if the need arises to chase a suspect." His gaze dropped to his crutch. "I'm kind of hampered in that department right now."

"You're not wrong. We'll see how things go. Take care. Don't leave your seat unless you really have to. Ring me if necessary."

"Seems too lazy to me. I'll see how I go."

Sam waited until the door eventually closed behind him and picked up her phone to call James's uncle, Raymond Campbell.

The secretary put her on hold for a brief moment, and then the man's stern voice came on the line.

"Hello, sir. Sorry to interrupt you. I'm the Senior Investigating Officer in charge of your nephew's case and wondered if you had time for a quick chat with me."

"Well, I'm under the cosh, as you can imagine, what with James not being here. But I'll do my best to help where I can."

"Thank you. This morning I've spoken with Vanessa

Farrar and your brother and I wondered if you might be able to fill in any blanks for me."

"Blanks? I'm not sure what you mean."

"We're trying to ascertain if James has had to possibly deal with any trouble or negativity in the weeks leading up to his disappearance."

"Let me think, are you referring to his daily role here? Is that what you're getting at?"

"Yes, can you recall anything untoward happening that you think might help the investigation?"

"Not really. If there was anything, he didn't tell me. What are you saying? That you think this is a deliberate act? That Lorna and James have been abducted?"

"Possibly. It's hard to tell at present, with very few clues to go on. So we need to cover every angle with our questioning."

"I'm not aware of anything, but then, I've been away for a few weeks. Only got back from the Maldives on Saturday myself. Hence me sounding stressed, having to deal with the backlog of work. Would you like me to have a chat with our junior associate and see what she can tell me?"

"If you wouldn't mind. Do you want me to stay on the line or would you rather call me back?"

"I'll call you back as soon as I've spoken to Cathy. Let me have your number, will you?"

Sam gave him her details and hung up. She twiddled with her pen while she patiently awaited his return call. Her phone rang ten minutes later. "DI Sam Cobbs, how may I help you?"

"Hello, it's me again, Inspector, Raymond Campbell."

"Hi, thanks for getting back to me. How did you get on?"

"Nothing I'm afraid. Cathy said James kept the ship upright all week without any problems. I'm afraid that's going to be no help to your investigation, is it?"

"Sadly not. Has he ever had a problem with a client?"

Silence as he considered her question. "No, not that I can recall. He's very easy to talk to and shows our clients sympathy when they need it. It can be a very stressful time for some people, dealing with their accounts, such a lot at stake where their business acumen is concerned."

"I understand. Oh well, it was worth a try. Thank you for speaking to me at such short notice."

"My pleasure. Where does that leave the investigation now?"

"We have a few leads to keep us occupied for a little while, don't worry."

"Oh, I see. That sounds hopeful. The sooner we have Lorna and James back the better. All this is a grave concern for both families."

"I can imagine. We're going to do our best for you all. Goodbye, sir."

"Goodbye, Inspector."

Sam ended the call and replaced the phone in its docking station. At the same time, her mobile vibrated across the desk. Des's name filled the tiny screen. "Hi, Des, what do you have for me?"

Her pathologist friend cleared his throat. "I'm aware that you've taken on the case of the burnt-out vehicle and the driver going missing, along with his girlfriend."

"Get on with it, man. What do I need to know?"

"We managed to get inside the vehicle and have a good look around. In the footwells at the front we found two mobile phones."

"Two of them? Tell me you can obtain some information from them, or am I asking the impossible?"

"We're dealing with them now. Don't raise your hopes, they're burnt to a crisp. I just wanted to let you know. You can always get in touch with their service provider, but you know that, right? I'll be in touch soon."

Then he hung up on her.

She held the phone away and shook her head. "And goodbye to you, too."

CHAPTER 2

"So what plans do you have for the weekend?" Michelle asked her boyfriend. She glanced around at the stunning scenery.

He hooked an arm around her shoulder. "I thought we might spend the entire weekend in bed, together."

Michelle slapped a hand on his chest and giggled. "You've got a dirt-track mind that seriously needs cleaning up, Grant Adams."

"Ah, it has been said before, and many have tried and failed to clean up my behaviour."

Her mouth gaped open, and she stared at him. "Go on, rub my nose in it. I know I'm not your first but do I have to keep reminding you that it's not cool to continually mention your past conquests?"

Grant stopped and laughed. She wrenched out of his grasp.

"I was hardly doing that. Six months we've been going out together. In my book, that's a long time. But if you continue to be sensitive about 'my past conquests', I truly can't see a way forward for us."

Michelle glared at him and stormed off. The car park was a few hundred yards away. Within a few strides he'd caught up with her.

"Leave me alone, you insensitive pig. If you want to call it off, it's fine by me."

He stopped again and stated sternly, "You're going over the top about this, Shell."

She turned to face him and through gritted teeth said, "Am I? You make me sick to my stomach sometimes. Think you're a great catch for most girls, well, not this one, not any more. I can't stand to be around you any longer."

He stood there and laughed. "I take it you won't be wanting a lift home then."

"Screw you, arsehole. I'll hitch a ride if I have to."

"Be my guest." He started walking and breezed past her.

She stared after him, aware she didn't have the guts to hitch a ride alone. Reluctantly, she dragged her feet and joined him at the car. He was inside, just sitting there. Their gazes met, and he smiled.

He opened the car door and shouted, "Looks like we'll both be hitching a ride, the bloody car is dead. And don't go off on one, it is what it is, and there's nowt I can do about it as I don't know the first thing about what goes on under the bonnet."

"I wasn't going to have a go. What about your breakdown service, can you ring them?"

He averted his gaze to the fields surrounding them and to the hills beyond. "Umm… it ran out last month, and I forgot to renew it when payday came around. You know how it is."

"Bloody hell, how irresponsible of you, and no, I have no idea how that goes because I always set aside funds for the necessities in life, such as keeping my car fully operational and on the road at all times."

"And I can do without a lecture from you, thanks all the same."

"Bloody charming, that is." She removed her rucksack and slumped against the side of the car. "What do you propose we do now, then?"

He glanced around and spotted a van in the corner of the car park with two people inside. "I'm going to be cheeky and try and cadge a lift. Wait here."

Grant sprinted the width of the gravelled area and tapped on the driver's window. The driver lowered it, and they had a brief conversation. Then Grant and the driver, who had a bad limp, came back to Grant's car.

"This is Vic, he's handy with cars and has offered to take a look for us."

"That will be brilliant, thanks so much," Michelle gushed, excited to get the car fixed and on the road again, especially as it was already nine in the evening.

The man tinkered with different elements and sighed a lot while Grant and Michelle peered over his shoulder.

"That doesn't sound too good," she said.

"It's not. I've tried everything I can think of, but nothing has made a difference. You can give it a go, but I doubt if she'll spark into life," Vic told Grant.

Grant jumped in and turned the key. Nothing but silence. He smacked his hand against the steering wheel.

Michelle gave him a warning glance, silently telling him to calm down. "Oh no, what do you suggest we do now? It's getting late."

"The breakdown services work twenty-four hours a day. Just ring the one you're registered with," the man offered helpfully.

Grant joined them. "A slight problem there. Mine ran out last month, and I kind of forgot to renew the policy."

"Ouch! Then I suppose you're screwed, mate, aren't you?"
Vic chortled.

"I don't suppose you would be able to give us a lift, would
you?"

"Depends on where you're going."

"Umm… Windermere," Michelle said.

The man winced and sucked in a breath. "Wrong direction for me, love. Sorry. I'll tell you what, I've got a mate
who's a mechanic. Let me give him a call, see if he can come
out and rescue you. It might cost you a bit, though, just to
warn you."

"It doesn't matter, Grant has saved money not buying his
breakdown policy anyway," Michelle grumbled, firing off the
angry jibe.

"All right, Shell, give it a rest. Bitching at me ain't gonna
solve the problem."

Michelle's head dropped. There was no point bleating on
about the mishap now, it was over and done with. She forced
out a mumbled apology. "I'm sorry."

"Can you give your mate a call for me, Vic? I'd really
appreciate it."

Vic nodded and walked a few feet away from them to
make the call. "Hey, Barry, yeah, it's Vic. How's it hanging,
pal?" Vic laughed and peered over his shoulder at them and
shrugged. "Yeah, as much as I'd love to catch up with you,
mate, I'm calling to ask a favour… I've got a couple of friends
in desperate need… yeah, their car has broken down… I
know it's late, that's where the favour comes in… any chance
you can come out and get it going again for them? They're
eager to get home… nah, they're not up for spending a night
in a hotel… nope, it ran out last month… yeah, I thought the
same, nothing we can do about that, mate, is there? You
will…? That's great news. Yeah, take your time, we can stay
with them, maybe take them to the pub up the road while we

wait for you to come out. Come straight to the car park and give me a shout when you get here. Cheers, you're the best. See you soon, pal." He ended the call and limped back to them. He thumped his leg. "Damn thing has gone to sleep on me again."

"What happened? To your leg?" Grant enquired.

"Grant! Don't be so nosey. It's okay, Vic, you don't have to tell us."

"It's fine. I was in the army, took a bullet in the leg out in Afghanistan during the conflict."

"Ouch. Is it still in there?" Grant asked.

"Yep, it's caught up in the nerves. The hospital said it would be too dangerous to take it out. Either that or I lose the leg. I didn't fancy being legless, not in that respect." Vic guffawed.

"Oh, fair enough," Grant replied. "Umm... is your mate coming out?"

"Yep, he's just about to tuck into his dinner. The missus will have a fit if he hits the road now. I've told him we'll wait in the pub for him. Come on, let's not hang around out here."

"We can't thank you enough for going the extra mile for us," Grant said. He locked the car and walked after Vic, leaving Michelle standing there.

Letting out an exaggerated huff, she had to jog to catch up with them. "Thanks."

Grant frowned and turned her way. "For what? Give it a rest, Shell, I've had as much crap as I can deal with from you today, you hear me?"

"You won't hear another word out of me, ever," she bit back childishly.

"Now, now, children. Don't let the situation be the cause of you two falling out."

"We won't. The relationship was dodgy to begin with, has been for a few months," Grant muttered.

47

Michelle stopped and shouted after him, "That's bloody news to me, Grant Adams."

Both men stared at her, and tears dripped onto her cheeks. The day was turning into a disaster through no fault of her own.

They reached the van, and Vic offered to take Michelle's rucksack that she had brought with her. Grant had apparently already put his in the boot and hadn't bothered to take hers from her. In a way, she was grateful, it had all her possessions in there. Her phone, makeup, comb, perfume, everything but her complete wardrobe.

Vic put the rucksack in the rear and opened the back door on the passenger side for Michelle to climb in. "This is April. I think you're going to get along well."

"Hi. I'm Michelle. I can't thank you both enough for coming to our rescue like this. I hope we're not putting you out?"

"You're not, don't worry. We're happy to help a damsel in distress."

They both smiled, and the men jumped into the two seats at the front.

"How's the leg doing, love?" April reached a hand over and rested it on her partner's shoulder.

"Better if we don't talk about it, sweetheart. It'll be fine now I'm sitting down again. Off to the pub we go then. Have you guys eaten today?"

"I had something at lunchtime. I would have normally eaten by now, but Grant suggested we eat after climbing the fell. I could eat a horse."

"No doubt I'll be able to force something down my neck," Grant added.

The van fired into life, and the tyres squealed as Vic tore out of the car park in a hurry. "Sorry, damn leg, I thought I had control over it, I guess not. All right if we go to the Green Man Inn?"

"Never been there myself, is it good?" Grant asked.

"Yep, best pub for food in the area in my opinion. Ain't it, April?"

"It is, Vic. I'd love to go there, if everyone else is up for it."

"Suits me," Michelle said. "As long as it has a welcoming atmosphere, they serve coffee and excellent food, then I'm a happy bunny."

"All of the above and more," April replied. "It's a lovely pub, you'll enjoy it."

Michelle relaxed back into her seat and smiled at their good fortune of finding such a kind couple who were willing to go above and beyond to help them.

The pub came into view up ahead.

"Ah, yes, I've passed this so many times but I've never been inside. Shame on me." Just then Michelle's stomach rumbled. "I'm so sorry, how rude of me."

April tittered. "No need to apologise, our bodies always show us up when we least expect it. Come on, let's go inside and grab a table. Leave the men to lock up the vehicle." Once they had exited the vehicle, April slipped her arm through Michelle's, and they entered the pub. "I need to nip to the loo first."

"I'll come with you," Michelle said.

The toilet was clean and smelt of orange blossom from the fragrance sticks positioned on the shelf above the sinks. "Wow, these loos are amazing. What a welcome. If the loos are like this, I can only imagine what other luxuries await us."

"You're in for a real treat."

April entered the first cubicle, and Michelle took the one next door. A few minutes later, they re-emerged and washed their hands with the lavender soap.

After drying her hands under the high-speed drier, April ran a comb through her long brown hair.

Michelle watched, admiring the woman's perfect high cheeks and the slimness of her elegant neck. "You're beautiful. Oh my, did I say that out loud? I'm so sorry."

April flipped her hair over her right shoulder and grinned. "Compliments are always gratefully received. I don't tend to get many from Vic."

"That's a shame."

"What about you and Grant? How does he treat you, Michelle?"

"On occasions he can be the perfect gentleman. You're not seeing the best side of him today. When he gets in a mood, everyone needs to watch out, not just me. As you're strangers, I think he'll be on his best behaviour tonight. I'm hoping that will be the case."

"You've had a stressful day. I suppose he's entitled to be a little grouchy."

"Maybe. I'm starving. What's the service like around here?"

"We usually get our meals within fifteen minutes, so not too long."

"What do you recommend? I always struggle to know what to have at a new place."

"Either the lasagne or the moussaka would be my choice."

"Lasagne it is then. I hope the others decide swiftly, I'm bloody starving, I am."

"I know Vic will. So the onus lies with Grant. What are you going to have to drink?"

"Just a coffee, an Americano will do."

"I always have the same, less calories. Us girls need to think of our figures, don't we?"

Michelle rolled her eyes. "Every hour of every day, or so it seems. You're nice and slim. Do you exercise much?"

They left the toilet and continued their conversation on the way to the table the guys had found close to the large open fireplace that lay unlit due to it being the height of summer.

"I walk the fells when I can and also do some wild water swimming occasionally," April informed her.

"Oh heck. I couldn't do that. Swimming in a warm pool is my limit."

"Scaredy cat. It's invigorating," April said.

"What is?" Vic asked. He patted the chair beside him, and April slipped into it.

Michelle smiled at the couple who were clearly in love, then sat in the seat next to Grant. He inched away from her when her arm accidently touched his on the table. *Up yours, Grant.*

"We've already decided what we're having," April told Vic. "Lasagne for both of us. What about you?"

"I'm torn between the steak and ale pie and the haddock and chips. What about you, Grant?"

"Steak and ale pie sounds great to me."

"That's settled then. I'll place the order and get the drinks in. Pint of bitter or lager for you, Grant?"

"Lager. I'll come with you. This is on me this evening, just to show how much I appreciate your coming to our rescue."

"I'll settle up with you later," Michelle called after him, but he chose to ignore her.

"Oops, I see what you mean about his bad mood," April said.

Michelle sighed. "I think this will be our final meal together."

"Your last supper, eh?" April chuckled. "You'll be fine. You both need to take a step back and process things. He's let you down, but it's a minor let-down really, isn't it? It's not like he intentionally broke down."

"I suppose you're right. I'm just sick of his attitude towards me most of the time. I try to do my best, but it never seems to be good enough for him."

"Hey, that's men for you. Vic is no angel, I can assure you. His leg plays him up something chronic at times, and he often snaps at me for no reason. I just brush it off and get on with my life. It's hard, relationships are always fraught and filled with compromise most days, don't you agree?"

"I guess so." Michelle waved her hand. "Hey, ignore me. The last thing I want to do is put a dampener on the evening."

The men returned, sharing a joke.

"That sounds unreal, a blast even," Grant said. He set the cutlery on the table in front of each of them.

"It was. You'll have to try it one day," Vic agreed. He winced as he retook his seat.

April rubbed his thigh and pecked him on the cheek.

"What are you talking about?" Michelle asked, keen not to be left out of the conversation and seeking to get back into Grant's good books after April's pep talk.

"Internal sky diving. Apparently, there's a place up the road that does it."

Afraid of heights, Michelle shuddered. Walking the fells had taken a lot of getting used to when she'd first begun trekking up some of the more dangerous peaks, but she'd gradually overcome her fear in the end. "Not sure I could do it."

"Why?" April asked.

"I have a fear of heights," Michelle replied.

"Yeah, and don't I know it? You've held me back the last six months. Friends of mine have taken on the Wainwright challenge in the last few months, slowly working their way through it, but misery guts here put her foot down when they took on the steeper ones."

Michelle's temper got the better of her. She slapped him around the face and then bit down on her lip.

"That's the first and last time you ever strike me, bitch. We're through, I mean it."

"I'm sorry. You've pushed me too far today. Regarding the challenge, you've got a tongue in your head, if you wanted to go without me, you only had to tell me."

"What? And put up with you being in a strop all day? No, thanks, not worth the hassle. Anyway, I can make up for lost time from now on. The guys won't mind retracing their steps and going round a second time, that's what we do for each other, we're not selfish, never have been. Unlike some I could mention."

Michelle left the table and ran into the ladies' toilet. The tears flowed freely, and she stood in front of the mirror staring at her reflection. Cursing herself for ever agreeing to go out with Grant.

"Hey, are you okay? That was uncalled for back there. I feel for you," April said, warmth evident in her sympathetic words.

"He's changed recently. He's not the man I first agreed to go out with. I can't stand him belittling me in front of you guys, who are, let's face it, virtual strangers to us. Don't get me wrong, I'm grateful for what you're doing for us, but…"

"There's no need for you to point that out. We're here for you. Come on, don't let him get to you. The second you walked away from the table you could tell he regretted his harsh words. Now dry your eyes and go back in there with your head held high. It's what we women do. Don't let the fuckers, with the dangly bit between their legs, grind you down."

Michelle covered her face with her hands and then released them. "You're right. You're such a wise woman. I guess I haven't had that many relationships to know how to

53

handle these moody men. It would appear I have a lot to learn in this life."

"It's a never-ending undertaking. I can tell he's not the right guy for you. I must admit, I was tempted to reach out and slap the shit out of him back there, as well. I restrained myself admirably, I can tell you. You don't need a man disrespecting you like that, love."

"I know. I won't allow it to happen any more. Thanks for your kind words. You've come to my rescue for the second time this evening. You're amazing."

"Not at all. I'm just older and a little wiser than you are, lovely. Now dry your eyes and let's go."

April led the way back to the table. She shielded Michelle from Grant. She sat next to him. He leaned over and whispered an abrupt apology in her ear. She pulled away from him, couldn't bear the thought of him being within spitting distance of her. He took the hint and shifted away from her in his seat. Michelle glanced up and spotted Vic and April eyeing her with empathy.

The waitress arrived not long after and deposited their meals. For some reason, Michelle's appetite had dwindled rapidly since Grant had placed the order. She picked at her meal while the other three ravenously tucked into theirs.

She managed to finish a quarter of the lasagne. Grant mumbled something indecipherable when he collected her plate and piled it on top of his own.

"What about a pudding?" April asked.

Michelle cradled a hand over her stomach. "I'm full. I couldn't possibly eat anything else. Don't let me stop you from enjoying yourselves, though."

"We won't. Actually, I've had enough myself," Grant said. He glanced at his watch. "Your mate should be arriving soon, shouldn't he, Vic?"

Vic twisted his wrist to note the time and nodded. "Soon

enough. We'll give it another ten minutes and then trundle back to your car."

April smiled at Michelle. "I'll be sad when this evening is over. I feel we've bonded as a group. Not sure that's ever happened before, has it, Vic?"

"Not to my knowledge, love. We do seem to have hit it off. Maybe we could arrange to meet up again… under less stressful circumstances. What do you say, guys?" His gaze drifted from Grant over to the agitated Michelle.

She shrugged. "Not my decision, it's down to Grant."

He stared at her and mimicked her shrug then took a sip from his pint, leaving the question unanswered.

April gathered Michelle's hand in hers and leaned in to whisper, "Who cares about the men, we can still meet up for a coffee and a natter somewhere, can't we?"

"I'd love that."

"What job do you have?"

"We're both graphic designers at the same company." Michelle faced April and rolled her eyes.

"Oh, how interesting. Is it?"

"I think so," Michelle replied.

"It has its moments," Grant muttered, his grumpiness palpable.

"Come now, you love it normally, Grant," Michelle taunted. "Maybe it's the thought of working alongside me you can no longer handle." She narrowed her eyes, probing for his reaction.

He took another sip and finished off his drink. "Pack it in. I won't warn you again, Shell."

"Bugger off with your threats, Grant. It's not my fault your bloody car broke down."

He stormed out of the pub, and Vic went after him. "Leave him to me."

April shook her head. "Do you think you're going to be able to get past this issue?"

Michelle tutted. "I doubt it. I've witnessed it before, when he's fallen out with someone at work, there's no reasoning with him. I haven't got it in me to try either. What's the point? Life's too short to tiptoe on eggshells all the time, isn't it?"

"I couldn't agree more. Have you finished? Maybe we should make a move before he kicks off again."

"Yeah, I'm ready. I hope Vic's mate can get the car going again."

"He will. He's the best mechanic this side of the Pennines. It's you I'm worried about. My heart is breaking for what is going on between you. No one could have foreseen this happening. You guys should be sticking together, instead you're being forced apart."

"It's him. He needs to buck up his ideas, not me."

They left the pub and walked towards the van. The men weren't around, so Michelle assumed they were already inside, waiting for her and April. Michelle opened the back door to see Vic in the front seat, Grant nowhere to be seen. "Where is he? I didn't see him come back in the pub."

"Get in. He started back on foot, said he wasn't prepared to wait a moment longer. We'll pick him up en route."

April and Michelle settled into the back seats and attached their seatbelts.

"Everything all right, Vic?" April asked.

Vic glanced in his rear-view mirror and smiled. "Could be better."

The van set off.

Michelle searched the road ahead, puzzled that she hadn't spotted Grant yet. "He's not here. Could he have taken a shortcut? I suppose there are plenty of footpaths around the lake here."

"Yes, he mentioned something about doing that," Vic said. "We're nearly there now. Don't fret, we'll catch up with him soon."

They pulled into the car park and drew up alongside Grant's car. She shifted in her seat to view all the different paths that led back to the area and couldn't see Grant anywhere. Michelle turned back to face April and discovered both her and Vic staring at her. Something about the way they were appraising her gave her the willies.

"What's going on? What have you done with Grant?"

Vic tipped his head back and let out a sinister, foreboding laugh. "You'll find out soon enough. Do the deed, April."

Before Michelle had a chance to react, April bashed her on the temple with a heavy object, not once, but twice in quick succession, knocking her out cold.

CHAPTER 3

The postman dropped an unwelcome letter through Sam's door. She stared at it with a mixture of reluctance and interest surging through her. Rhys had just left for the day after stopping over for the night, missing the post by seconds. She was all alone now, just her and Sonny, her furry companion, sitting by her feet, waiting for her to put his lead on.

"I get the hint. This can wait, your bladder can't. Come on, tinker, off we go." She tucked the letter behind the picture of Sonny on the console table and gathered her light-weight jacket and Sonny's lead from the coatrack. It was a chilly June morning, and the grey clouds approaching from the east were a stark warning that rain was on the way.

Once they were ready, they left the house and walked the half a mile circuit around the nearby estate. Sam stopped on the edge of the green at the end and let Sonny off to do his business. Then she called him back and they headed home. On the way, she had one thing clawing at her mind, the official-looking letter she had put aside.

Back home, the confounded letter drew her attention like a magnet. After removing Sonny's lead, she collected the envelope and took it through to the kitchen. She opened it while the kettle boiled and her breakfast cooked. She could do without this crap on a Friday morning. Withdrawing the letter, she read the contents, all the while shaking her head as the words blurred before her eyes. Wiping away the tears of frustration that had come to the surface, Sam growled when the toaster popped up and the kettle switched off. Not that she fancied any breakfast now. She poured herself a cup of coffee and ended up throwing her toast in the bin, her appetite long departed and unlikely to return.

Therefore, our client is requesting that you sell the property and the proceeds to be shared fifty-fifty with him.

"Yeah, and you, Mr Archer, can go fuck yourself. Sorry if that doesn't sound ladylike to you, but it's the best I can do at short notice, replying to a shock of this magnitude. I have no intention of either selling this house or handing over fifty percent of the proceeds to my ex, who has saddled me with a bunch of debts." She was tempted to screw the papers up and throw them in the bin but resisted that particular urge at the last minute. In the end, Sam left the papers on the kitchen table and tried to ignore them as she fed Sonny and gathered his things together, ready to take him next door to Doreen.

However, the letter was always there, drawing her attention. She tucked it between the cruet set, she would deal with it later.

"Are you ready for the off, boy?"

Sonny raced to the front door and sat there, staring up at his lead again. It gladdened her heart to see him eager to commence his daily adventure with their neighbour. *That reminds me, I must pick up a box of chocolates or a plant for Doreen on the way home to show my appreciation.*

Doreen was at her lounge window, waiting for them to arrive. Sam waved and opened the gate. She let Sonny off the lead. He trotted up the path and sat patiently at the front door.

Her neighbour welcomed them with one of her brightest smiles. "You're early today. Everything all right, Sam?"

"Sorry, I never even looked at the time. Do you want me to take him home again, Doreen?"

"Don't be silly, it makes no odds to me. I was just making sure everything was okay with you."

Sam smiled. "As well as can be expected. You might as well know. I've had a letter from Chris's solicitor demanding that I sell the house and we split the proceeds fifty-fifty."

"What utter nonsense. That young man needs his head read if he thinks you're going to do that. You're not, are you?"

"Not if I can help it. I haven't told you this, but Chris lumbered me with a few debts. He forced me to take a couple of loans out in my name during the renovations, never contributed towards the repayments either."

"Wow, I had no idea. What an awful man he's turned out to be. You're better off without him, love."

Sam exhaled a large breath. "I know I am."

Doreen cleared her throat. "I don't have much, but I do have a couple of thousand sitting in the bank if you're desperate. I'm only offering it to you because I know I can trust you to pay it back."

Sam's eyes enlarged, and her cheeks heated. "You're so sweet. I appreciate the offer but I'll be fine, I promise. I truly didn't mean to burden you with my problems."

"You haven't. Don't ever think that, Sam. I'm always here for you. A problem shared and all that."

"It works both ways, Doreen. If ever you need anything, from advice to something that needs repairing around the house, you only have to shout. I owe you a lot for caring for

Sonny during the day for me as it is. I dread to think where we'd be if you hadn't suggested looking after him while I'm at work."

"He's family, you're family, well, to me you are. It's always a pleasure to have his company during the day. I just wish I was more agile and able to walk more then we could go off on little adventures of our own."

"Honestly, it's fine. I enjoy our walks before and after work, it helps to clear my mind."

"I thought as much. You have such a stressful job, dear."

Sam glanced at her wrist. "Speaking of which, I suppose I'd better get a move on. Here's what he needs during the day. I'm trying him on a different food. One packet at lunchtime with just a handful of his biscuits, if that's okay?"

"It is. Don't fret about us. You get off and catch some of those nasty criminals I keep hearing about on the news. Are you busy this week or is that a silly question?"

"So-so, we're dealing with a missing person case, two actually, boyfriend and girlfriend. I can't say much, but the girl has diabetes, hence her parents being concerned about her welfare."

"Oh dear, yes, I've heard diabetics need to be extra careful with how they eat throughout the day."

"Yes, it's true. Which is why we're pulling out all the stops and doing our best to find these people. Not having much luck so far, though, it has to be said. Have a good day, the pair of you."

"Oh, we will. And I hope your day improves considerably, Sam. Don't let the solicitor's letter get you down, sweetheart."

"I won't. It's already forgotten about, I promise. Thanks for taking such good care of my baby, Doreen. You know how much it means to me."

"I do. Enough said. Now be off with you."

Sam leaned forward and kissed Doreen on the cheek then ran up the path and jumped into her car. A note tucked under her windscreen wiper made her pause for a moment or two. She removed the note and opened it slowly.

Thank you for another perfect evening. I'll give you a call later. Rhys. X

Her heart fluttered, and she smiled. He was such an adorable man. Sometimes she needed to pinch herself to confirm all of this wasn't a dream.

She drove to the station on a high but with a niggling of doubt lurking somewhere in the shadows. Did she deserve Rhys? There were days when she wondered if he was too good for her and other days when she was glad to have him beside her on this journey called life. But the fear was always there, at the back of her mind, whether she'd do something to mess things up, like she had with her disastrous marriage... *No, that wasn't down to me. He wrecked our marriage by sleeping with that other woman.*

Bob was getting out of his car when she arrived. Her assistance was called for yet again to ease his effort, and they entered the station together.

"You seem a bit distant this morning, is everything all right?" he asked.

"I suppose you'd call it reflective. Let me get a couple of cups of caffeine inside me and we'll have a chat then, okay?"

"If you're sure."

Sam pushed open the door to the incident room and was surprised to find the rest of the team already hard at it. She stopped off at the drinks station and poured herself and Bob a coffee then she went through to her office to deal with her usual morning ritual of sifting through emails and letters, mostly from HQ. Her phone rang not long after she had settled at her desk. It was Nick, the desk sergeant.

"Sorry to interrupt, ma'am. I've just had word about

another missing person case, or should I say cases. A young couple who appeared to have vanished in the last couple of days. Thought you might be interested."

"Shit! Really? It's not like we've made much headway with the other case yet. Always tricky when someone goes missing without any clues to latch on to. Our frustration level on this one is at its highest. Can you drop the relevant information up to me, Nick?"

"On my way."

Sam ended the call and expelled a lungful of air. Nick knocked on the door a few minutes later and handed her a sheet of paper with the names of the two missing persons: Grant Adams and Michelle Barnes. "Grant's car was found in the car park at Grasmere on Thursday morning. No sign of the couple."

"Is that it?"

Nick shrugged. "Afraid so, ma'am."

"Who reported them missing?"

"Sorry, yes, I should have written that down. Michelle's parents. I'll get the info for you, knew I'd forget something today."

Sam frowned. "This is unlike you, Nick, everything all right?"

"The wife is going to the doctor's today. She's been having severe headaches for the past month. I suppose I'm more worried about her than I thought I was."

"Damn, so sorry to hear that. Try not to worry too much, it might not be anything serious."

"Believe me, I keep telling myself that, but it festers, doesn't it?"

"I know. Let me know what the outcome is."

"I don't want to involve you with what's going on in our miserable lives, ma'am."

"You're not. I'm genuinely interested."

Nick smiled. "It's true what they say about you, you're one in a million."

Sam laughed. "One snippet of character assessment going around, we won't mention the rest of it."

Nick left the office, and Sam used his absence to answer yet another email that needed her immediate attention, according to the subject. The desk sergeant rang seconds later.

"I have the contact details for you, ma'am."

"Let me get a pen and paper. Okay, shoot."

"It's Tricia and Tim Barnes. They live out in Windermere."

"Blimey, that'll take us a while to get there. I'll make contact via phone first. Have you got a number for me?"

He gave her the mother's mobile details and ended the call.

Sam immediately dialled the number. "Hello, is that Mrs Barnes?"

"It is. Who are you?" The woman sounded a tad wary to Sam's ear.

"I'm DI Sam Cobbs. I believe you just called the station to inform us that your daughter has gone missing, along with her boyfriend, is that correct?"

"Oh right. Yes, I'm so thankful for you ringing back so soon. Can you help us find them?"

"First things first, when did they go missing?"

"Wednesday evening. We've tried finding them ourselves, been out there day and night, but nothing."

"Am I to believe Grant's car was found at Grasmere, in the car park there?"

"Yes, that's right. They went for a hike after work, nothing unusual about that and, well, they never came home. What's surprising is that neither of them has tried to make contact with us."

"And they're generally reliable, is that what you're telling me?"

"Yes, extremely. Very responsible adults. Will you help us?"

"I think we should meet up face to face, if that's all right with you?"

"Yes. Do you want me to come there?"

"No. My partner and I will come to you. Are you at home?"

"I should be at work but I've taken a few days off because I'm so worried. How long will you be? Will you come today?"

"However long it takes us to get there. We'll be setting off as soon as I end this call."

"That's such a relief, I can't thank you enough for taking me seriously. I know my daughter well, and I can't shake off this feeling that something bad has happened to her."

"Please, try not to worry. Will you give us a couple of hours to get there?"

"Of course. You have my address, don't you?"

"Yes, I have it here."

"I'll see you soon, and thank you, Inspector Cobbs."

"You can thank me when we've located your daughter."

THE DRIVE HADN'T TAKEN them as long as Sam had anticipated. "Why come to us and not get the locals involved?" Bob grumbled.

She helped him out of the car and tutted. "Stop whining. I'm glad she came to us if this case is connected to the ongoing investigation we're dealing with. Put a smile on that dour face of yours."

"Charming. What if I don't feel like smiling, have you considered that?"

"I wish you'd told me back at the station how argumentative you were feeling today, I could have brought someone else with me instead."

"I'm not argumentative. Talk about kicking a man when he's down."

Sam stared at him. "I wasn't aware that I had. Can we stop this now? Go in there with clear minds and a willingness to help this poor woman to find her daughter?"

"Just the daughter, or are you going to include the boyfriend in the investigation as well?"

"Pack it in, Bob. You knew exactly what I meant, you don't have to nitpick every damn detail I mention." She stormed ahead of him and rang the bell of the large Georgian house situated in a small cul-de-sac.

"Nice house," Bob muttered in her ear.

The chain was removed from the other side of the door, and a smartly dressed woman in an edge-to-edge jacket that Sam recognised as a Chanel suit stood there, her face etched with concern.

Sam showed her ID.

The woman took it, studied the warrant card in detail and handed it back to her. "Thank you so much for coming. The traffic wasn't too bad then? Mind you, we're not in the heart of the summer season yet. The roads are always chocka during July, August and September. Horrible for the locals to put up with."

"The only real downside to living in a beautiful part of the country, eh?"

"It is. Sorry, do come in. You'll be wanting a drink after your journey. Tea or coffee?"

"Two coffees, one sugar and milk, if you don't mind? You have a wonderful home. Have you been here long?"

"Around twenty years. We love it here. Good neighbours who are worth their weight in gold. We have no plans to move anytime soon, despite the influx of visitors we get each year."

She showed them through to a huge kitchen, dining room and lounge all in one at the rear of the house, overlooking the garden. Beyond the boundaries were open fields and a view of the hills in the distance.

"What an exceptional vista you have to suffer every day." Sam laughed.

"Yes, it definitely enhances our lives. Take a seat on the sofa. Are you warm enough? It's a bit damp today. I can turn the heating on if you prefer?"

"We're fine. Unless you want it on."

"No. I'll get a thicker jumper if I need it. Both my husband and I are usually out at work all day, so we don't tend to put the heating on until we get home. I try to stick with that routine." She poured the drinks and carried them to the coffee table on a wooden tray. "I'm so upset, you're going to have to forgive me if I break down now and again."

"Don't worry, it's to be expected. Can you give us a little background information on your daughter and her boyfriend?"

"They've been going out for around six months. They get on well together, often go up the lower fells either at the weekend or after work, providing the weather is in their favour. That's where they went on Wednesday. It was a beautiful evening, so they took off. We haven't seen or heard from either of them since. I'm very concerned for their safety. I don't know what to think. I've been in touch with the Mountain Rescue; they've searched the area, had the helicopter up there and found nothing. It's just not like Michelle not to contact us. I'm trying desperately not to think of all the bad things that might have happened to them but, I have to tell you, I'm struggling."

"That's understandable. I hate to ask the obvious, but have you contacted her friends to see if anyone else has heard from them?"

"Yes, we've done all of that, and so have Grant's mum and dad, and still nothing. Two people go missing, and they fail to contact anyone via their phones... in this day and age, it just doesn't ring true to me."

"You have a valid point. What about their jobs, have you rung their bosses, seen if they've shown up at work?"

"Yes, I've done all that. They work together at a graphic design firm just down the road from here. The last their colleagues saw of them was when they left work on Wednesday and headed over to Grasmere. I'm sorry, but you're going to have to take my word that I've tried everyone and anyone who I think they would be in touch with and, well, I've drawn a huge blank."

"I'm sorry to upset you, I have to cover every little detail."

"You haven't. I'm just finding all this rather overwhelming. It's the not knowing that is my greatest worry."

"Is either of them sick? Do they have any illnesses or chronic conditions that might need monitoring that we should be aware of?"

Mrs Barnes frowned and ran a hand over her face. "No, they're both very healthy, hence their love of challenging themselves on these long hikes. Not something I've ever relished doing in my younger days. Is there a specific reason you asked that question?"

Sam snuck a quick glance in her partner's direction. He must have sensed her looking his way and raised his head from the notes he was jotting down. Their gazes met, and he blinked a few times and gave a brief nod, letting her know he agreed she should mention what was on her mind.

"Inspector? Your silence is beginning to make me

anxious. If you know something, don't you think I have a right to know?"

"You do. I don't usually do this sort of thing so early into an investigation, but I think this case warrants it."

"Warrants what? You're not making any sense."

"Unfortunately, this is the second case of this kind we've come across this week."

Mrs Barnes gasped, and her hand slapped against her cheek. "Are you telling me that another young couple has gone missing?"

"Yes. They were reported missing on Tuesday. Of course, at this stage, it could be classed as a coincidence, given that we have no evidence linking the two cases, but I'm willing to put my neck on the line and link them."

Mrs Barnes sat back and shook her head. "This is incredible. Hard to believe that this could be happening. Are you suggesting that someone might be targeting young people with the intention of kidnapping them?"

"Possibly. Again, we don't want to speculate too much because that can often cloud our judgement during an investigation."

"The other couple... are they from wealthy families?"

Sam sucked in a breath and let it pass through her lips slowly and nodded. "Yes, fairly well off. It seems vulgar to say that, I'm sorry."

"If it's the truth then there is really no reason for you to apologise." Mrs Barnes's hand shook as she ran it around her face. "I feel absolutely numb. I just don't know what to make of this revelation. I think my husband should be here. He's so much better at this type of thing than I am. Would you mind if I give him a call?"

"Not at all, please do."

She left her seat and ventured into the hallway. Sam

strained her ear and listened to the woman talking on the phone in the distance.

"Now you've told her, what next?" Bob whispered.

"The truth?" she asked.

He nodded.

"I don't know," she said. "Maybe her husband will be able to supply us with a possible lead to investigate. We're scrabbling around in the dark as it is."

"That's the understatement of the bloody century."

Mrs Barnes's heels click-clacked in the hallway, and Sam placed a finger to her lips, silencing her partner.

"He's coming straight home. Just to warn you, he might be a touch angry when he gets here. Tim hates it when I disturb his working day."

"This is an important issue, though, I'm sure he won't mind."

"We'll see soon enough. His office is only two minutes down the road."

"What does your husband do?"

"He's a solicitor."

Sam chewed on her lip.

"Is there something wrong, Inspector?" Mrs Barnes promptly asked.

"It might be nothing, but the fathers of the other young couple are both solicitors."

"What? I can't believe what you're telling me."

The conversation came to an abrupt halt when the front door slammed. Heavy footsteps came their way and, before long, a large man with grey hair filled the doorway.

Mrs Barnes burst into tears the second she laid eyes on her husband. He rushed into the kitchen and threw an arm around her shoulder.

"It's all right, Tricia, I'm here now. She's going to be all right. We need to remain strong, we spoke about this last night, didn't we? After we heard back from the rescue team."

"But you haven't heard what I've just heard, Tim."

He sat in the chair next to his wife and held her hand tightly. "Would someone care to enlighten me? Sorry, you are?"

Sam slipped her hand into her pocket and extracted her ID. "DI Sam Cobbs, and this is my partner, DS Bob Jones. Nice to meet you, Mr Barnes, thank you for coming home to be with your wife."

"Yes, yes. Just tell me what's going on here."

"Your wife has gone through the sequence of events leading up to your daughter's and her boyfriend's disappearance. I've just informed her that this is the second case of this nature we're handling this week."

"No! Are you telling me that you believe my daughter and Grant have been kidnapped?"

"Possibly. We have another young couple reported missing at the beginning of the week. They had also been walking on the fells. The only difference that I can see so far is that their car was found in a Keswick car park, burnt out."

He shook his head and ran a hand through his already spiky hair. "I'm not sure I'm liking the sound of this."

"Sorry, I know all this is upsetting for both of you, but the more facts we gather, the more chances we have of finding them."

"Tell him what you told me before he came home," Mrs Barnes said through her tears.

"We think we've just uncovered a possible connection."

"Which is?" he asked brusquely.

"Both fathers of the other missing couple are solicitors."

His head jutted forward, and he held Sam's gaze for several uncomfortable moments. Eventually, he said, "That's some coincidence, don't you think?"

"We'll definitely be beginning our investigation with that in mind, sir. I have to ask if you've had any cases lately where the client either got irate or took umbrage with any advice you have issued."

His lips distorted as he contemplated his answer. "Not off the top of my head, no. Saying that, it's possible. As solicitors we tend to turn people's worlds on their heads, that alone can cause a lot of internal conflict that fails to show itself in my office. If that makes sense?"

"It does. Can you think of anyone who you might have unknowingly upset recently, sir?"

"No. I'll need to sit down and think about that one. I can't believe any of my clients would take umbrage and then purposefully go out and abduct my daughter, that's just sick."

Sam shrugged. "Unfortunately, sometimes desperate people do desperate things to get their voices heard. I'm not saying that's what has happened here, but it's something we need to consider all the same."

"I can understand. Let me put my thinking cap on and let you know, maybe later today. My mind is spinning as if it has been caught up in the tail end of a tornado right now. Do you have a card?"

Sam withdrew two from her jacket pocket and slid them across the table towards the couple. "Is there anything else you think we should know? Has your daughter fallen out with anyone at work or maybe one of her friends lately?"

The couple looked at each other and shook their heads.

"No one who would go to the extremes of kidnapping her, if that's what you're asking," Mr Barnes replied.

"You mentioned your daughter and Grant are both graphic designers. Can you give us the name of the firm they work for? We'll drop by and have a word with their boss before we head back to Workington."

"Scenic Designs in Windermere, on Windsor Avenue. I'll

look up the postcode if you're not familiar with the area." Mr Barnes touched the screen on his mobile, tapped in his passcode and angled the phone in Bob's direction so he could jot down the information.

"Thanks, that's a huge help," Bob said.

"Would I know the other families involved?" Mr Barnes asked.

Sam flipped open her notebook and read out the names of the two fathers of the first missing couple. "Oscar Farrar and Patrick Campbell."

He glanced at the wall off to the right and thought for a second or two. "No, I can't say I recognise either of their names. Sorry."

"It's okay. It was a long shot. Maybe we are dealing with two similar but unrelated investigations within the same week by pure coincidence then." Sam smiled. Inside, her stomach was churning with uncertainty. "We're going to head off now."

"What will you do now?" Mrs Barnes asked.

"We'll go to Grasmere, have a root around over there, and then go back to the station to get the ball rolling. We won't stop until we find the answers we're seeking, I promise you."

"That's reassuring. I hope something comes to light soon," Mrs Barnes said, a sob catching in her throat as the tears welled up.

"There, there, don't go getting yourself upset again, love," her husband chipped in. He patted her hand, and she offered him a weak smile. "I'm sure we're in safe hands with the inspector here."

"Thank you for having confidence in our abilities. We're going to do our very best not to let you down. Should Michelle contact you, or anyone else for that matter, will you ring me right away?"

"You have my word. Are you hinting at some kind of ransom demand?"

His wife gasped again, and her husband's arm snaked around her shoulders.

"Possibly, it's something we should be prepared for." Sam rose from her chair. She turned to her partner and offered him a hand to get to his feet.

"Oh dear, accident or an operation to put something right?" Mr Barnes asked.

"I had an argument with a van during our last investigation," Bob replied.

"See, just goes to prove how much we put our lives on the line for our victims' families," Sam added.

Mr Barnes tilted his head and asked, "Did you find the person responsible?"

"Oh yes, the gang are all behind bars now. Although, it was touch and go for a while there. We managed to arrest them in the end, no lives lost, which was an added bonus." As soon as the words left her mouth, Sam cringed. "Sorry, I shouldn't have said that. Ignore me."

"That's difficult to do in the circumstances, Inspector."

"Again, I can only apologise. I meant nothing by my flippant remark. Going back to Grant's car, was it? It was found in Grasmere. Can you give me the exact location?"

Mr Barnes picked up his phone and brought up a map. He gave them the postcode of the car park, and Bob jotted it in his notebook.

"Is the car still there or has someone else collected it?"

Mr Barnes sighed. "We decided it would be best to leave it there, in case either of them showed up. We didn't really know what to do for the best between us, if I'm honest."

"I think you've made the right call. Maybe Michelle or Grant will find their way back to the vehicle. Do they both have a set of keys to it?"

"No. Only Grant."

"Okay. We'll take a ride over there and have a nose around. Thank you for sparing the time to see us, Mr Barnes. Try not to worry too much. I know that's going to be an impossible task for both of you. You have my assurances that my team are the best around. Our record is second to none."

"That's just what we needed to hear. Will you keep us up to date with your progress?" Mr Barnes rose from his seat and made his way towards the front door.

Sam and Bob followed at a steady pace, given Bob's predicament.

At the door, Mr Barnes shook their hands and lowered his voice. "Please tell me what our chances are of seeing our daughter again."

"You mustn't think like that, sir. Try and remain positive at all times. We're going to do our best not to let you down."

"Thank you. I foresee a few sleepless nights ahead for both of us until Michelle is back where she belongs, here with us."

After reassuring the couple endlessly during their conversation, Sam couldn't summon up any other words of comfort for him. "We'll be in touch soon. Take care of each other."

"We will. Thank you again, Inspector. Good luck with the investigation. She means the absolute world to both of us."

Sam nodded and left the house. She paused outside while Bob struggled down the steps. They crossed the gravelled drive, and Sam opened the passenger door for Bob to get in.

"You're treating me like an invalid, and I hate it."

"Stop whining. You should be grateful, most men would relish the thought of their boss mollycoddling them."

He stared up at her from his seat and said crabbily, "I doubt if that's true."

Sam slammed the door shut, sniggered and ran around the front of the car to the driver's side.

"What did you make of them?" Bob asked.

Sam started the engine and pulled away from the house. "Nice couple. Not deserving of what is happening to them. What was your perception of them?"

"The same, sort of. Strange that three of the parents are all solicitors, ain't it?"

"Isn't it," she corrected him.

"Whatever. I only say it because I know how much it winds you up." He laughed, and she thumped him in the thigh—luckily, it was his good thigh.

"Ouch. What was that for? Don't bother replying, I think I can guess."

"Why ask then? Damn, I need to go back."

"What for?"

"I forgot to get a photo of the daughter."

"It would help."

She turned the car around and pulled up outside the house. Mr Barnes had just left the house, presumably on his way back to work.

"Is something wrong?" he asked, frowning.

"I forgot to ask for a recent photo of your daughter. If you have one of her and Grant, even better."

"Let me see if Tricia can help you with that." He opened the front door and bellowed for his wife to join them and to bring her phone with her.

Tricia Barnes appeared moments later. "What is it? Oh, hello again, Inspector. Has something happened?"

"She wants a recent photo of both of them. I thought you'd be the most likely to have one."

"Of course. I took one on Saturday when they were both here before they went out for drinks with a few of their friends." She scrolled through her photos and handed the phone to Sam. "Is this one any good?"

"Yes, that's perfect. Can you send it to my mobile?" Sam

churned out the number, and Tricia tapped it into her phone and sent the photo.

Sam's phone tinkled, indicating that she had received the message, and she smiled her appreciation at the couple. "Thanks. I'll be in touch soon." She ran back to the car and left the drive again.

"Fancy you forgetting that," Bob mumbled.

"Fancy you not thinking to remind me before we left the house."

"Touché."

"Right, now the recriminations are out of the way, what's your take on things?"

"What's to say that hasn't already been said? Are we talking about these kids, or should I say these young adults, going missing because they've been abducted by someone? If so, whom and why?"

"That's exactly it, isn't it? All solicitors' children as well. That has to be a significant fact to the investigations, doesn't it?"

"Yeah, of course, it depends on what type of solicitors we're dealing with here. Do they work in the same field or different ones?"

"Get onto Claire, ask her to do some digging for us. Get her to trawl through the archives, see if any of the names have been in the headlines lately and, if so, for what?"

Bob placed the call while Sam drove to the address Mr Barnes had given her for the graphic design workshop. Sam instructed Bob to stay in the car while she went inside to question the staff. Everyone was appalled that Grant and Michelle were both on the missing list, but no one could furnish Sam with any reason why someone would want to hurt them. She left the studio half an hour later. When she returned to the car, she caught Bob dozing in the front seat.

She battered the bonnet with her clenched fist, and he jumped a mile.

She laughed and could have sworn he mouthed the word *bitch* at her. "Sorry, I couldn't resist it. You've got a bloody cheek having a snooze while I'm slogging my guts out."

"Hardly. You've never done a day's manual work in your life."

"Sod you, matey. What did Claire have to say?"

"Claire's going to look each of the solicitors up. Nothing came to mind with her. She's usually pretty knowledgeable about things in the press like this."

"Yeah, I know she is. She's the office oracle. I wish I had more of her ilk on the team."

He yawned and stretched out the crick in his neck. "Jesus, don't you ever give it a rest? You're always thinking of some way of having a pop at me."

Sam grinned. "Ooo... you do have a sensitive nature today, don't you?"

"Yeah, so stop trying to push my buttons."

"Get you. For your information, I wasn't. Let's not fall out about this, Bob. I have enough shit on my plate to deal with already without us being at loggerheads."

"Sorry. I didn't think. Do you want to talk about it? I'm happy to listen."

"You have enough crap of your own to deal with right now. I'll be fine."

"I insist. If I can help, I will. Yes, I'm a touch incapacitated at present, but..."

"All right, you asked." She put her foot down on the open road towards Grasmere. "I received a letter from his nibs' solicitor this morning, demanding that I sell the house and split the proceeds fifty-fifty."

"Fucking shit, he is. What's wrong with him? Want me to

go round there and give him a good talking-to, with my crutch?"

Sam laughed, summoning up the scene in her mind. "No, the last thing you need is an assault charge to add to your problems. I'll handle it, somehow. I won't take it lying down, that's for definite."

"I know you won't. I'm always here if you want to bounce any ideas off me. I know you have a new man in your life now, but I'm still around if you want to run anything past me."

"I know you are. Umm... Rhys doesn't know yet. The letter arrived after he left for work."

"The relationship is ticking along nicely then if he's stopping over most nights now."

"I suppose so." Her cheeks warmed under his gaze.

"Sorry, I didn't mean to embarrass you. I'm glad you're happy with him. He sounds a decent bloke, unlike the other fucker. God, the day I saw Chris coming out of that slapper's house, well, I could have killed him. Some men are gutless shits. Can't stand it when they cheat on their wives. I'm ranting now, sorry."

"You're not. I'm glad I've got you and the rest of the team in my corner. You've all been brilliant throughout this ordeal."

"We're family, not just work colleagues. Most of us. That Alex is a weird one, but every family has a dysfunctional member to keep them on their toes, right?"

Sam chuckled. "I'm going to tell him you said that."

"You dare. I hear he's got a mean right hook on him."

"Okay, maybe I'll reconsider, just to keep the peace. How are things at home? You know, living with a hormonal teenager in the house."

"Thankfully, Milly's been behaving herself lately. Abigail is under stress at work still, what with the Covid rates on the rise again. Stupid government shouldn't have relaxed all the restrictions."

"I agree. Although anyone who seems to be catching it now tends to get over it fairly quickly."

"I think other grave news is keeping the statistics from hitting the headlines. Abigail tells me that people are still losing their lives due to the disease."

"It's all doom and gloom everywhere, isn't it?"

"Looking back, nothing has really changed. We all find something to bitch about, don't we?"

"True enough."

Bob spent the next thirty minutes recanting tales Abigail had told him regarding her shifts at the hospital, some of which had Sam in fits. Like the time a porter was transferring a shrouded body via the lift used by visitors rather than the staff lift that had broken down. The thing was, the body rose, scaring the shit out of the three visitors and the porter. The doors opened not long after, and all the passengers legged it and ran screaming along the corridor. The story didn't end there, though, because the stiff on the trolley turned out to be another porter who had decided to play a practical joke on his colleague. Both porters ended up being reprimanded after the visitors who had got caught up in the prank had called the hospital to raise a complaint.

By this time Sam had tears streaming down her cheeks. "Oh God, I need the bloody loo now."

"Eww... too much information, boss. Glad I achieved something."

She gave him a puzzled glance and quickly returned her gaze to the road again. "What are you talking about?"

"At least I brightened your day up for you."

"Bob, somehow, whether intentionally or not, you always manage to do that. Right, this is the car park. Wait, are those the public loos over there?"

"Yep."

Sam parked in a free space and yanked on the handbrake. "I'll be two ticks." She bolted out of the car and into the loo only to find there was a fifty-pence charge to use it. "Bloody daylight robbery."

"You're inside the national park, love, get used to paying for the privilege to be here," a voice from one of the cubicles called out.

"I need to fetch some change. I hope I don't wet myself in the meantime."

The woman chuckled.

Sam returned to the car, and Bob stared at her.

"That was quick," he said. "Did you wash your hands properly? You know, sing 'Happy Birthday' a couple of times?"

"Up yours. I need fifty pence to spend a penny, if you get what I mean."

Bob dug into his trouser pocket and pulled out a handful of change. "Will two twenties and a ten be all right?"

"You're a lifesaver. I'll pay you back later."

"I'll hold you to that."

She ran back to the toilet, popped the change into the turnstile just inside the main door and eventually made it to the vacant cubicle before she had an accident. Her relief was profound. When she came out, the mystery woman was rubbing her hands together under the drier.

"You made it in time then?"

"Only just. How long has the turnstile been in operation?"

"Not sure, maybe a couple of years."

"Ludicrous. Can't see the point of charging fifty pence myself, not when there are quite a few pubs around where you can have a pee for free."

"It's criminal, that's what it is," the woman said. "There's never a copper around when you need one."

Sam continued to wash her hands at the sink and hoped the rising colour in her cheeks didn't give her away. "Absolutely, shameful, it is. Nice to meet you." Sam moved over to the drier, but the woman wasn't going anywhere anytime soon.

She leaned against the wall and continued to rant about everything she detested in the summertime when the masses descended upon the area. "It's the little louts I abhor the most. They come to this region to experience the beautiful surroundings and yet they don't take their litter away with them. It's disgusting and disrespectful."

"I totally agree. The litter situation in this country is way out of hand, especially around here."

"Maybe we should all write to our MPs. Ha, on second thoughts, they're just as useless. And don't get me started on the lockdown parties that were held at Number Ten. My father died in hospital of Covid, and none of us were allowed to be there for him. He was an exceedingly popular man who had fought for his country, and at the funeral, only fifteen people could attend. Crucified me that did." She wiped away the tears that had emerged. "That PM of ours has a lot to answer for in my opinion. He should never be in power. A man who can't find a decent barber should be ashamed of himself. He's a buffoon, an utter moron. Oh, and another thing, I'm really wound up now, the bloody energy crisis we're all going through all because the government refuses to dish out windfall taxes on the energy companies. Now every last one of us has to pay for their corrupt short-sightedness." The woman shuddered and drew in an extra breath. "Anyway, I can't stand around here all day putting the world to rights. Enjoy the rest of your day, dear. It was nice to meet you."

Sam smiled and followed the woman out of the toilet, hoping she didn't get stuck in the damn turnstile on the way out. She bid the woman farewell at the door and jumped back in the car beside her partner. "Sorry for the delay. I got held up listening to that woman droning on about this, that and the other. If one more person mentions the energy crisis to me again… I'm going to slit my wrists."

"You need to brush up on your tactfulness to get out of predicaments like that. I always have an excuse ready on the tip of my tongue."

"That's because you're super organised where avoidance tactics are concerned. I hear enough excuses from you every day to know that."

He opened his mouth to dispute the claim, but she held a hand up to stop him.

"My ears are still painful from that woman battering them, I can do without you adding to my misery."

He crossed his arms and sank lower into the seat. "Bloody charming. After all I do for you, you fling this shit at me."

Sam leaned over and pinched his cheek. "You know I'm only messing with you. Stop taking things so seriously. Right, back to the case in hand. We've got their vehicle parked here, out in the open for everyone else to see."

He frowned. "Yeah, and your point is?"

"I suppose what I'm suggesting is that someone could have easily swooped down and abducted them. All right, it's busy now, but would the car park be that busy later on in the day, in the evening?"

Bob shrugged. "I have no idea. I don't come out this way much. We need to find a local to provide us with an answer to that one."

Sam turned in her seat and looked at the houses at the end of the road and the pub they had passed on their way there. "We could ask at the pub."

"Sounds like a good idea. While you ask the questions, I could down a sneaky pint."

"Not going to happen on my watch, matey. I'll treat you to a coffee instead, how about that?"

"If you insist."

Sam started the engine and drew away.

"Just thinking outside the box a bit here, hear me out," Bob said. "What if their car had broken down and they went to the pub seeking help?"

Sam's brain went into overdrive. "Maybe, it's a definite possibility. Let's see what we can find out."

After parking the car in the Green Man Inn's car park, Sam helped Bob out of the car, and they entered the public lounge.

"You take a seat. I'll get the coffees in. Do you want a sandwich while we're here? My treat, it must be getting close to lunchtime by now." She glanced up at the clock behind the bar. It was twelve-fifteen.

"That's kind of you, boss. Remind me to give you fifty pence for the loo again sometime."

Sam tutted. "What do you want?"

"Ham and cheese on white if they have it, and a white coffee, thanks."

Sam approached the amenable barmaid.

A nametag with *Katrina* typed on it was pinned to her right breast. "Hi, what can I get you?"

"Hi, Katrina, do you have a menu?"

She turned, took a laminated card from the shelf behind and handed it to Sam. "There you go. Anything and everything on there from jacket spuds to sandwiches to steak and chips to chicken wrapped in Parma ham."

"Blimey, don't tempt me. I think a sandwich will do."

"On the other side. Can I get you a drink while you decide?"

"Two white coffees, thanks. Right, one ham and cheese

84

sandwich on white for my partner, and I'll have a tuna and mayo on brown."

"Very well. I'll bring them over. That's fourteen twenty."

Sam handed over the money and scanned the pub. She noticed CCTV cameras in a couple of corners but said nothing and returned to sit with Bob.

"Did you ask?"

"Not yet, you impatient bugger. I thought I'd place the order first and then dive in with the questions when the barmaid brings us our lunch."

"Ah, okay. Makes sense."

She leaned forward and said, "Here's some news for you… everything I say and do makes sense, partner."

He snorted. "If you say so."

The barmaid brought their lunch around ten minutes later. "Can I get you anything else?" Katrina asked.

"A little information perhaps," Sam said.

Katrina seemed perplexed. "I'll do my best."

"What's it like around here in the evenings, is it busy?"

"It can be. It's mostly dependent on the weather. May I ask why?"

Sam produced her ID. "We're investigating a case of two young people going missing in the area. That's as much as I can tell you at the moment."

"That's a shame. When did they go missing?"

"We believe they came to Grasmere on Wednesday evening. They parked in the car park over the road there, and their car is still there. Neither family has heard from them since. They walked the fells in the area late Wednesday afternoon."

"Could they have had an accident up on the hills? Have you considered that? Not heard of anyone going missing around here, not in that sense. We hear about the occasional accident happening up on the fells, you know, people panicking and calling the Mountain Rescue Team for assistance, but I can't say I've ever heard of anyone going missing. Are you sure that's what has happened?"

"The family seems to think so. The rescue team was dispatched, and they found nothing up there."

"How strange."

Sam nodded. "I was wondering if I showed you a picture of the two people concerned whether you might recognise them."

"I can try. I'm usually pretty good with faces."

Sam withdrew her phone and scrolled through her messages to find the relevant photo. She showed the barmaid who took her phone for a closer look.

Katrina nodded slowly, her nod gaining momentum. "Yes, I remember them. They were in here with another couple."

"Really? That's brilliant. Umm... I noticed you have some cameras dotted around the bar, do they work?"

Katrina laughed. "Of course they do, what would be the point in having them if they didn't?"

"You'd be surprised just how many pubs have them only as show, to act as a deterrent."

"That's shocking. Nope, Ian insists we run this place properly from washing the glasses to switching out the discs every day for the CCTV. Do you want me to have a word with him? He's in the office dealing with some paperwork. I'm sure he'll be happy to help you out."

"Fantastic. Thanks very much."

"Not a problem. I'll have a chat with him and send him over to you once you've had your lunch."

"Any time is fine by me." Sam sank her teeth into her sandwich as Katrina walked away from them. "This is good," she said to her partner.

"Mine's delicious. Shame it's so far from the station, I'd be happy to nip in here regularly when we're out and about."

"It's reasonable, too. Let's hope we walk away with more than a satisfying lunch under our belts."

"Here's hoping, it sounds promising," Bob agreed. He tore into his sandwich, and a dot of butter oozed out and landed on his chin. He grabbed his serviette and wiped it.

"You're such a messy eater."

They ate their meals and drank their coffee. All the time, Sam anxiously glanced over at the bar, awaiting Ian's arrival. Finally, after Sam had downed the last of her coffee, he appeared behind the bar. Katrina pointed in their direction, and he came over to speak with them.

"Hi, Katrina told me you wanted a word."

Sam invited him to take a seat and ran through what she wanted.

He sat on the nearby stool and leaned forward. "I see. I can certainly have a gander for you to see what I can find. Do you want another coffee while you wait? On the house, of course."

"That'd be great. Thanks so much."

He rose from the table and went back to the bar to instruct Katrina. She smiled over at Sam and raised her thumb.

"Nice couple," Bob acknowledged.

"You're only saying that because you're getting a freebie out of them."

He grinned. "True. I'm parched for some reason today, so another coffee is a welcome addition."

Katrina brought their drinks and removed their dirty plates and cups at the same time. "Was everything all right?"

"It was lovely. Great food topped off with fantastic service. Thanks for the second coffee, it's appreciated."

"You're welcome. Ian shouldn't be too long. He's a typical bloke, he gets distracted easily."

"We're in no rush. Well, within reason, so don't fret about it."

Ian reappeared at the end of the bar and gestured for Sam to join him. "You stay here and enjoy your coffee," she told Bob.

"I intend to," he replied.

She followed Ian through the bar and up a small corridor to his office at the rear of the building. "This place is huge. Do you own it?"

"Yes. Touch and go there for a while whether we shut the place down or not due to the blasted pandemic, but I made significant cuts to the staff, and now we manage to scrape by, just."

"Not telling you how to run your business in the slightest, but I would definitely consider putting your prices up. You're too cheap. If the public loos across the road can charge fifty pence for a wee, then you should be charging more than you are for a sandwich. It's great quality, I'm sure your punters wouldn't mind paying the extra."

"You're very kind. I'm glad you enjoyed it. Maybe we should consider putting the prices up at certain times of the year, to capitalise on the tourists being around. I'll have a serious think about that. It's a fine line, I wouldn't want to piss anyone off."

"I hear you. I should imagine running a pub is a devil of a job sometimes, but then, you have rising costs to cover yourself, have you thought about that?"

"It's a constant reminder. I need to grow a pair and do as you suggest, raise my prices. Anyway, enough about my struggles. Let's see if we can help you obtain the information you need."

"Did you locate the couple on the footage?"

"I found a snippet of two couples sitting at a table. They shared a meal together and appeared to be getting on well, as though they were good friends, until one of the couples seemed to fall out with each other."

"Interesting. Can I take a peek?"

He played the disc, and Sam found herself fascinated by the interaction between the couples from the first frame.

"They do appear to know each other very well."

"That's what I gathered from observing them. I'll fast forward a little, see what you make of this."

It wasn't long before an argument seemed to kick off between Grant and Michelle before she slapped him. The other couple looked uncomfortable at the table when Michelle left it and went towards the toilet. Not long after, the other woman followed her into the ladies'.

"Hmm... very interesting. Can you give me a copy of this?"

"Of course. I'll do that for you now."

"What about the cameras outside? Do they work?"

"Yes, absolutely. I didn't bother with them. Let me get this copied for you first, and then we can see if we can find anything else from the ones outside."

She watched him take a disc from its case, insert it into the machine and hit the Record button. Then, on another screen, he ran the footage highlighting outside the pub.

"Let's see what we can figure out from this one, shall we?"

Sam inched closer to the screen. Ian whizzed through the footage and located the time the foursome left the pub.

"Excellent," she said, "at least we've got a good image of the four from this angle."

"Yes, it's all fine and dandy here, but I suspect it's all going to go downhill outside."

"What makes you say that?"

He sighed. "I keep saying I'm going to renew the cameras outside. They're lacking the quality of the ones inside, you'll see that for yourself soon enough."

Sam watched the two couples leave the pub which was fine, but as Ian predicted, the quality diminished rapidly the farther they got from the pub. "Ouch, this isn't so good. Are they heading towards that black van?"

"Yes, I think so. I'll try and fiddle with the controls, see if I can get the image clearer, but I'm not holding out much hope."

He didn't succeed. But something of importance did catch Sam's attention. "There. The man is at the back of the van with Grant. Did he just clobber him?" Grant toppled and the other man pushed him into the back of the vehicle.

"Yes, he hit him over the head, at least that's what it looked like to me."

"Grainy picture or not, it's there for all to see."

Ian continued playing the disc, and Sam watched Michelle and the other woman leave the pub and hop in the back seats of the van. The van then drove out of the car park.

"Bugger, we can't make out the number plate, can we?" Sam said.

"Sorry, that's as good as it gets."

"Damn. Never mind. You've done your absolute best for me, that's all I can ask."

"Sorry, wish the news was better. I feel like I've let you down at the most important time."

"Please, don't think that. Maybe if I drop it off at the forensics lab, they'll be able to enhance the picture, enabling us to at least get a partial number plate. I can't thank you enough for the evidence you've been able to provide us with so far."

"I hope it helps your investigation. It's all I have at this stage. What I can do is distribute the image of the two couples to the rest of the staff, and if either of them enters the pub in the future, we could get in touch with you right away, how's that?"

"I was about to suggest the same. You've been super help-ful. I feel confident something good will come from the footage."

He smiled, pressed the Eject button on the machine and removed the disc. He handed the case to Sam. "I hope it makes a difference to your investigation. Hate the thought of someone being up to no good around here."

"Me, too. I'm sure we'll find the couple we're searching for soon, thanks to the evidence you've just supplied." She waved the disc.

Ian nodded and led her back through the pub to Bob who was chatting to Katrina at the bar.

"Any good?" he asked.

Sam smiled and took a gulp of her lukewarm coffee. "Yes, I think so. We'd better get on the road again. Thanks for all your help." Sam smiled at Ian and Katrina.

Bob hopped down off the stool and winced. "Ouch, I knew I was chancing my luck getting up there."

Sam rolled her eyes at the couple behind the bar. "It's not easy working alongside this clown every day, I can tell you. Come on Hopalong Cassidy."

The bar erupted as Sam and Bob left the pub.

"Did you have to embarrass me like that?" he said.

"Umm... I didn't, I think you'll find you embarrassed yourself by trying to chat up the barmaid. Tell me I'm wrong."

"You're way off the mark with that assumption. I'm hurt you should think that of me."

"I'm sorry. I withdraw my accusation. Can we get back to the station now? Actually, I need to drop something off at the lab on the way back."

"Are you going to tell me what you found out?"

"In the car. Get in. Do you need a hand?"

"Nope. I've got this."

Sam waited in the car, revving the engine impatiently while he dropped into his seat and tucked his crutch into the footwell.

Once they were on the road again, Bob asked, "Go on, are you going to reveal what you saw?"

"Four people, who gave the impression to outsiders they were old friends. I didn't get the idea they'd only just met."

"If they've been abducted then the kidnappers might have been putting on a show for anyone watching. Maybe they're sickos. They'd have to be, to go to a public place with someone they were intending to kidnap. Why take the risk of being caught on camera?"

"Yeah, on the other hand, perhaps they were so focussed on grabbing their victims the thought never occurred to them."

"Yeah, forgive me if I'm not buying that one. It's a risky strategy they took, why?"

"No idea. It's something we're going to have to work out for ourselves. The camera outside the pub managed to pick up the vehicle. It also captured the perp belting Grant who then fell into the rear of the van. The two women left the pub and jumped into the back seats, and they took off."

"Good, so if the camera picked up the van, we have a plate we can run then, right?"

"Not exactly. The images were very grainy. Hence our need to stop off at the lab en route."

"Ah, gotcha. That's a pain in the arse."

"Maybe. We'll see soon enough."

An hour later, Sam drew up outside the lab and left Bob in the car while she entered the building. The receptionist asked if she could help her. Sam explained the position she was in, and the receptionist placed a call to the relevant department.

A tech wearing a white coat joined Sam a few minutes

later. "Come with me. I'll run you off a copy. No doubt you'll be wanting the original for yourself."

She followed him the short distance down the corridor to an office. "Thanks. I didn't want to take the liberty of asking the landlord for two."

"Take a seat. I'll do it now for you."

"Much appreciated." Sam sat on the chair in the corner and ran through what she needed from the tech. He jotted her requirements down on his clipboard and copied the disc. Two minutes later, he handed her one of the discs.

"Is there anything else I can help you with?"

"No, thanks. Is Des around?"

"I spotted him earlier. He might be carrying out a post-mortem. Want me to give him a ring?"

"No. I know the way. I'll nip down there and have a word."

Sam walked the length of the long, grey, soulless corridor to Des's domain. She peered into his office to find it empty so continued to his main working area, or theatre as he preferred to call it, and looked through the window in the door.

Des happened to look up from the corpse he was cutting open and waved a bloody hand at her. She cringed and pulled a face at him then mouthed that she wished to speak with him, if he had the time.

His face expressionless, he left his position and crossed the room. She stood back as he pushed the door open with his elbow, his gloved hands held up in front of him.

"This had better be important, Inspector, I'm busy."

Fearing a backlash once she revealed why she was there, Sam's mouth twisted. "Umm... I was passing and thought I'd drop by and see how you were getting on."

His face told her that he knew she was lying. "Do you

want to try again? You have five seconds to spit out the truth."

"It's true, well, I needed one of the techs to enhance some CCTV footage for me and thought what the heck, I might as well drop by and have a quick chat with you."

"About?"

Sam tutted and puffed out her cheeks. "You have a really weird way of making me feel uncomfortable in my own shoes."

Des cracked a smile. "That's better than making you feel uncomfortable in your own underwear, I suppose."

She laughed. "An added bonus, I'll take that."

He tapped his foot and glanced at his bloody hands. "I'm eager to get back to the PM I was performing. Spill, Sam."

"If you insist. You know we're investigating the missing persons' case, and you're aware the young couple's car went up in flames at the beginning of the week."

He nodded.

"Bob and I have just come from Grasmere and before that Windermere…"

He gestured with his hand for her to stop prattling on and to get to the point.

"Well, the fact is, we have yet another couple who has been reported missing since Wednesday. Their car was located in Grasmere with no sign of them."

He frowned. "And your gut instinct is telling you that there is a connection between the two cases, is that it?"

"What? You think I'm wrong? Two couples go missing within the National Park limits, in the same week, and you think that's a coincidence?"

"I'm not saying that. I'm just advising that perhaps you need to be more cautious. The National Park is a pretty extensive area, people go missing here all the time through one reason or another."

Sam raised a pointed finger. "Stop. While I appreciate what you're saying, I truly don't believe that to be the case in this instance. Anyway, I think the disc I've just dropped off to the lab will substantiate my way of thinking."

"Job done then. Now can I get back to work?"

Sam's heart lurched. "I thought you'd be interested in what was going on, I was clearly wrong. I'm sorry to have bothered you, Doctor Markham."

"Ooo... get you. Don't go getting your hand up your arse about this, Inspector Cobbs. Come back to me when you have something of interest to go on, or if you find a dead body along the way."

Sam didn't bother responding. She turned on her heel and retraced her steps back to the exit, seething that he had dismissed her theory. Her cheeks inflamed, still showing evidence of her anger when she jumped back in the car alongside her partner.

"You look like you've gone into battle and been humiliated, am I right?" he asked.

"You could say that." Sam lashed out at the steering wheel. "I don't want to speak about it. I need to calm down before I have a conversation with anyone."

"And that includes me, does it? Fine by me, I'm all for a quiet life, you know that."

They continued the rest of the journey in silence and didn't speak again until Sam had parked up and was helping Bob out of the car. She mumbled an apology.

"What have you got to apologise for? I'm here if you need to have a chat. Someone has obviously upset you at the lab, you were fine before you set foot in that place, and yet you returned to the car with a face like thunder, therefore, I don't have to be a genius to figure out what's gone on."

"You're a good man, Bob Jones. I'm fine now. Let's move on and not dwell on it."

"Whatever works for you. The last thing I want to do is add to your stress."

"Thanks. Are you ready to go?"

He closed the passenger door and nodded.

Once they had returned to the incident room, Sam ordered Liam to get everyone a drink and asked them all to gather around while she brought the whiteboard up to date with the second missing couple's details. Bob made himself useful by inserting the disc in the machine, then he brought the TV to life with the remote control.

Everyone arranged their chairs in a semi-circle around Sam.

She took a sip of coffee and cleared her throat. "This is what we have on the couple so far. Michelle's mother told us that her daughter set off with her boyfriend late Wednesday afternoon for a hike around Grasmere. The boyfriend's car was located in one of the public car parks there. Bob and I took a punt and called at the nearest pub, closest to the car park, and showed the photo we had of the couple. To our amazement, the barmaid recognised them and told us that the couple had dined there on Wednesday evening, with another couple. Maybe they went hiking with someone they knew. I need to double-check that with Michelle's mother as I believe she was under the impression the couple had ventured out alone. Bob, can you run the disc for me?"

The image played on the screen. Sam pointed out Michelle and Grant. "This is the couple who has been reported missing. As you can see, everything is friendly enough between them until around halfway through the meal when Michelle and Grant appear to fall out over something. She slapped him and then stormed off to the ladies' loo."

"And the other woman goes with her, what, to comfort her?" Claire asked.

"So it would seem. When they return to the table, we see that Michelle has lost her appetite and avoids further eye contact with Grant until the four of them decide to leave."

"Do we know who paid the bill?" Liam asked.

Sam raised an eyebrow. "Good point, one I forgot to ask. Bob, will you ring the Green Man Inn after we've finished and find out?"

Bob nodded and made a note on his pad.

Sam continued. "The next clip is of the four of them leaving the pub. The two men leave first. This is where we pick up a dark van, either dark blue or black. I'm plumping that it's the latter, but I'm prepared to sit on the fence rather than narrow it down to the wrong colour and end up with egg on my face. The back of the van opens, and the perp clobbers Grant on the head. He topples into the rear, and then the two women leave the pub and walk towards the van. I'm surmising they believe both men are inside, waiting for them. And that, team, is all we have."

"In our favour, we do have a good picture of the four people," Suzanna said.

"We do, that's about all we have right now. My next step is to get a press conference organised, get the photos out there in the hope it will prevent anyone else from going missing."

"Are you saying you believe these two befriended Michelle and Grant with the intention of abducting them?" Claire asked.

Sam shrugged. "That's about it. It's not like we have anything else to go on right now."

"I suppose the key is going to be finding that van," Bob said. "Are you going to mention it in the press conference?"

"Should I? Yes, I think I will. As with all press conferences, I'll be taking a risk mentioning the vehicle and indeed putting the perps' faces out there for all to see. Let's hope it doesn't backfire and force them to do something major they later regret."

"Like kill the hostages, if they still have them," Alex replied.

Sam nodded. "Okay, folks, let's continue digging, it's all we can do until the lab gets back to us about the vehicle. In the meantime, I'll be in my office, organising the conference. Hopefully it won't be too late for Jackie to work her magic and get one arranged for today."

Sam entered her office and paused for a moment to take in the view of the hills she could see in the distance. *Such a beautiful place to live and for folks to visit. How can this be happening? People setting out to admire this wondrous landscape only for them to go missing. How? Why? Who the heck is behind something as devastating as this? What do they hope to achieve, abducting the couples?* She tried to push away the sinister thoughts she had after internally asking the last question and sat behind her desk to place the call.

"Hi, Jackie, it's yours truly, on the cadge as usual. How are you fixed today?"

"Hi, Sam. Ah, I have a bit of a backlog to deal with. I can probably organise something for you in the morning, if that's any good?"

"It'll have to do. I know you'd squeeze me if it were at all possible."

"I have time to discuss your needs now."

"That's great. I'd rather get it out of the way and get back to the investigation before the day is out. No dead bodies on this one, yet. During the last week, two couples have been reported missing in separate incidents. No connection between them, as far as we are aware. The latest couple to go missing were seen dining in a pub..." Sam paused when Bob appeared in the doorway. "Hold the line a sec, my partner needs a word." She covered the phone.

"I rang the pub, the bill was settled by Grant Adams."

"Great, okay, thanks, Bob. I'll be out soon."

Her partner hobbled out of the room, and Sam continued her conversation.

"Hi, I'm back. Sorry for the interruption, it was important to the case. As I was saying, the second couple, recently reported missing, was seen dining with a man and woman in a pub near to where their car was found abandoned. I've just received confirmation that the boyfriend, who has gone missing, paid for the meal."

"Interesting. And the couple they were eating with? What do you know about them?"

"We suspect they possibly went out of their way to befriend Grant and Michelle, maybe to abduct them."

"Bloody hell. Is that even a thing? Grr... ignore me, of course it is, I've been in this job long enough now to know that anything is possible these days with regard to criminals with agendas."

"Yep, you've got that right. Anyway, I want to hit this one hard and fast out of the traps. I'm going to show the public pictures of the two kidnappers and the vehicle they were driving on the night in question. Maybe it'll encourage someone to come forward and supply us with the names of these bastards. Excuse my language, but if these two people are up to what I suspect they're up to, well, they need to be caught ASAP."

"I agree. Let's see what we can do about that. Can you give me an hour to make the necessary arrangements for you?"

"Of course. Thanks, Jackie." Sam ended the call and then, for some reason, felt the need to speak with her sister. She rang the bridal shop to see if Crystal was available for a quick chat. "Hi, it's only me. Are you busy?"

"Hey, I was going to ring you later to see how the romance of the decade is going."

Sam laughed. "It's hardly that, love. Let's just say I'm extremely grateful for the choice I made."

"You definitely have a way with words. I'm so happy for you. Any word from the other fucker, I mean your ex, yet?"

"Something came in the post before I left for work this morning. It was from his solicitor. He's demanding the house be sold and the proceeds split fifty-fifty."

"Like that's going to happen after the loan debacle. What an utter shitbag he is. You're well shot of him. I know you know that, too, although it doesn't help the situation much, knowing that, does it?"

"Nope. I don't have any other option than to bow to his demands. I can't see any other way around it, Crystal."

"What? No way. I refuse to let you give in to him. If you need money, I have some set aside for my pension, we both have. Take it and pay him off. You can pay us back in the future, with interest if it'll make you feel any better."

Tears bulged, and Sam sniffled. "God, you're so kind, you're breaking my heart here. I couldn't possibly put either of you in that position. You've both worked hard for your money, I swear I wasn't hinting."

Crystal laughed. "I never thought you were. The offer is there if it'll prevent you from doing something you'll later regret. Fight him all the way, that's my advice. You have the law on your side. Screw him before he screws you, love. If you get my drift. What an absolute arsehole he is. He was never good enough for you. I always knew there was a slime-ball lurking beneath that smug exterior."

"You did? Why didn't you try to warn me then?"

"The same reason I wouldn't have listened to you if you had offered ill-timed advice on my relationship. Love is blind, remember."

Sam groaned. "I get that. What a bloody mess. I know everyone is in the same boat right now, with the cost of living going up. The truth is, I don't think my wages will cover everything plus an extra mortgage cost on top."

"It's appalling to see the state the country is in. I can see nothing but people getting into significant debt through no fault of their own. Ugh... don't get me started on the political side of things, nope, not going there. I get so wound up but, at the end of the day, what can we do about it? Sod all, that's what. The government is laughing at us, taxing the wrong people in this country. It's definitely a case of the rich getting richer."

"Umm... I thought you weren't going to go down the politics road."

"Yeah, well, it had to be said. It doesn't alter the fact that I have a significant lump sum put aside for my pension. If you need to dip into it to save yourself from ditching your lovely home, then my offer still stands."

"You truly are the best sister to ever walk this earth. So kind, understanding, generous..."

"Carry on, you're doing my ego the power of good. Honestly, I'm not doing anything that you wouldn't do for me, if the tables were turned, sweetheart. Right, I'm going to have to go, I have a bride and her mother due in five minutes. I'll give you a call later, and you can fill me in on all the juicy details about your illicit weekend away together."

"Nothing to tell. We went on long walks with the dogs and snuggled up by the fire in the evening. As far as telling you what went on in the bedroom, you're going to have to use that furtive imagination of yours."

"Spoilsport. Ring you later. Glad to hear you so happy, Sam."

"Thanks. Love you."

She ended the call, checked her emails, dealt with

anything that was urgent and then returned to see how her team was getting on. Jackie rang back within the hour, telling her that a press conference had been arranged for nine-thirty the following morning. Sam detested having conferences to deal with at that time of day, she'd need to begin her day earlier in order to be prepared. Great.

She worked her way around the room, starting with Claire. "What have you got for me?" Sam perched on the edge of a nearby desk and leaned forward.

"I did as Bob requested and rang all of the parents who are solicitors and sadly drew a blank. None of them know each other personally. They've vaguely heard of each other, but that's as far as it goes."

"That's strange then. Maybe it's a coincidence that the parents have the same careers."

Claire flattened and waved her hand from side to side. "I'm sorry, I'm just not buying that."

Sam heaved out a sigh. "Yeah, I'm not convinced by that belief either. But, if the couples have been specifically targeted because of who their parents are, then the kidnappers would have had to have been tracking their movements, wouldn't they?"

"Sounds plausible to me, boss."

"But if anything suspicious like that had presented itself in the past month or so, you know, either couple fearing they were being followed, none of the parents were aware of it. I asked them if anything untoward had surfaced, and both of the girls' mothers said no."

"Very curious. I'm at a loss as to what to suggest in that case, boss."

"Never mind, I'm sure something will surface soon enough for us to sink our teeth into."

Sam moved around the room. Alex had put himself in

charge of trying to locate the vehicle and was already pulling out what hair he had left. "Well?"

"Yes, thanks, boss. You know me, things rarely get me down."

Sam shook her head, couldn't help grinning. "Numpty. Go on, what can you tell me about the van?"

He pulled a face. "Not a lot is the easiest answer. Do you have any idea of the number of black vans there are in Cumbria?"

"I should imagine far less than white ones."

"Yeah, only just. There are thousands of the buggers. Without a plate to go on, the task is going to take me an eternity to get through."

"You volunteered to get stuck into this one. Are you telling me you no longer want to do it?"

"Hey, I didn't say that. I'm just warning you that it might take longer than anticipated to find the results we need."

"All I can ask is that you do your best, and hopefully, once the lab gets back to us, your job will become a lot easier. In the meantime, try and whittle the list down for me."

"Any suggestions how I should do that?"

Sam glanced in her partner's direction and glared at the smirk he was wearing. Then turned her attention back to Alex. "If you need me to tell you how to suck eggs, then here goes. First of all, I would search for all the black vans registered within the two immediate areas where our two couples have been reported missing. After that, I would extend the search and see how that turns out."

"I'll do it your way then. Thanks," he grumbled and fidgeted under her scrutinising gaze.

Sam decided to leave him to it and continued to work her way around the room, answering any likely queries the other members of the team had before she returned to her office where she made some notes for the conference being held the following morning.

Tiredness washed over her like a tsunami, and she ordered the team to pack up and leave at ten past six. On the drive home, she stopped off to buy a plant for Doreen and then continued her journey on autopilot. When she was almost home, Rhys called her.

"Hi, I'm in between patients. I know I said I'd be there at around seven this evening, but an emergency appointment was made by my secretary before I had the chance to ask her not to make any further bookings."

"Hey, that's not a problem. Honestly, I'm dead on my feet tonight, or I will be after I've taken Sonny for a walk and fixed his dinner."

"What are you saying? That you don't want me to drop by later, after work?"

She closed her eyes briefly and cringed, then swiftly opened them again when she realised she was still driving in heavy traffic. "Don't say it like that. Come round if you want to, however, I'm warning you there's a possibility I won't be good company this evening, plus I'll be setting my alarm for half an hour earlier in the morning, due to holding a conference at nine-thirty. On top of that, the rest of my evening is going to be taken up making endless notes in preparation for my battle with the press tomorrow."

"Okay, you win. I can take the hint... I'm kidding. Seriously, we should be able to tell one another the truth without coming up with a bunch of excuses as to why we can't see each other some evenings."

"I know. It's hard sometimes, letting my guard down and admitting my failings to you. Maybe I live in constant fear of not doing the right thing and am conscious of what might happen if I screw up."

"Idiot. You need to stop overthinking our relationship

and just go with the flow. I said from day one that I would never put pressure on you to do anything against your will. We're both up to our eyes in work most days. We're going to get the odd occasion when we need to put up our hands and admit we need a breather. You have my permission to do that without having to think up an excuse."

"But I wasn't making excuses. It's the truth, I'm likely to be lousy company this evening."

"There, that's sorted then. End of discussion. You do what you need to do and if you feel like having a chat later this evening, pick up the phone and call me. If you don't, then that's fine, too. Okay?"

Sam smiled and indicated right into her road. She groaned when she saw Chris's van parked outside her cottage.

"Everything all right?" Rhys asked, concerned.

"Yep, nothing I can't handle. I'm just pulling up outside the house. I'll definitely ring you later. What time will you be home?"

"Around eight-thirty, so not too late. Speak later. Take care."

"You, too. Bye."

Sam parked in her usual spot, and Chris appeared beside the driver's door within seconds. She lowered her window an inch to speak to him. "What do you want?" Her tongue swelled up when his name formed in her mouth so she avoided using it in case it choked her. She hated this man for what he was putting her through. Truly and vehemently *hated* him.

"Let's go in the house and talk like civilised people without the need for either of our solicitors to be present."

"Bollocks. I'm staying where I am."

He grabbed the door handle, but Sam was quicker and pressed the button on the armrest to lock the door.

"Now you're just being ridiculous," he said. "What? You think I'm going to hurt you, is that it? I've never laid a hand on you during our marriage."

"Who knows what you're capable of if you're angry enough? I've told you before, I never want to see you again, ever. I'm happy to leave any correspondence that needs to go on between us to our solicitors. Now bugger off and leave me alone."

He leaned against the side of the car and folded his arms. "I need some things from the house. Items I've bought. I'm not leaving here until I've got them."

Over the last month, he had been back and forth to collect his personal belongings so she knew he couldn't be talking about those. She stared ahead at Doreen's house. Her neighbour was standing at the lounge window with the phone to her ear. Sam wondered if Doreen was calling the police.

"Ignoring me isn't going to help, Sam. I have rights and I intend to exercise those rights."

She glanced up at him and shook her head. "You're out of your tiny mind if you think you're ever going to gain access to my house again."

"*Our* house, until the divorce goes through. I suggest you get your solicitor to run through what rights you have before you get yourself into any unnecessary bother."

"Two words… sod off."

Sam craned her neck at the sound of a siren heading their way. Her gaze was drawn back to Doreen who raised a thumb at her. A few seconds later, a patrol car appeared. Two uniformed officers exited the vehicle and walked towards them.

"I can't believe you called the cops," Chris groaned through gritted teeth.

"I didn't. I'm guessing Doreen did, worried that you were out here intimidating me."

"You bloody women always stick together. You won't get away with this, Sam. I'll make sure of that."

"Hello there, what appears to be the problem here? We've had a call that you're out here harassing this woman, sir, is that right?"

Sam purposefully kept quiet, hoping Chris would dig his own grave without any interference on her part.

"This woman is my wife. We're here having a pleasant chat, no aggro involved. I believe the neighbour may have just wasted your time, Officers."

"And what do you say to that, Miss?" the older male officer asked.

Sam smiled and placed her warrant card against the window for him to see.

The officer raised an eyebrow and inched closer to Chris. "Why don't you tell us the truth before you get yourself into hot water, sir?"

"How dare you? I am telling you the truth."

"If that's the case, then why has this lady locked herself in her car and is refusing to come out, even in our presence?"

"Because she's a drama queen," Chris growled.

"One more insulting word against the inspector and I'll arrest you for either harassment or disturbing the peace. I haven't quite worked out which of those offences would be appropriate."

"Neither. I haven't done anything wrong except show up here and ask her to hand over items from the house that belong to me."

The officer doing all the talking turned to Sam and asked, "Is this right, ma'am?"

"Over the last month or so he's taken all of his possessions. We're going through a divorce. I've asked him on more than one occasion to stop bothering me and to leave our solicitors to negotiate between them. I'm a busy woman and would rather not have to deal with all this hassle, Officer. He's aware of this and yet he still insists on coming here, making a show of himself. His tone was more aggressive this time, that's the reason I have remained in my vehicle. I've asked him to leave, and he has refused."

The officer nodded, and he turned to face Chris again with narrowed eyes. "I suppose you're about to dispute that."

Chris's chest inflated, and his cheeks were tinged with red patches. He shook his head and remarkably backed down. He shrugged and threw his arms out to the sides in defeat. "I give up. I'm never going to win this battle, your lot always stick together."

"Then my advice would be for you to go, sir, and don't come back. Leave the negotiations to your solicitors as the inspector has already suggested. Don't make matters worse. This type of situation can easily spiral out of control. It would be a shame if that were to happen and you ended up behind bars, wouldn't it, sir?"

"All right, I'm going." Chris launched himself off Sam's car and turned to wag a pointed finger at her. "You haven't heard the last about this, Sam."

The officer inched forward again and tutted at Chris. "Did I hear correctly? Did you just issue a threat, sir?"

Chris's anger was evident by now. He looked like a cartoon character. The only thing missing was the steam coming out of his ears. "I'm done here. I can't be bothered arguing the toss with you lot any longer."

Sam immediately felt triumphant as she watched him get in his van and drive away. She unlocked the door and got out. "I can't thank you enough. I believe if you hadn't shown up when you had, things would have got out of hand quickly."

"Glad to have been of assistance, ma'am. Any more hassle and you give us a call right away. That's our job, to prevent matters from getting out of hand, if possible. Are you going to be all right? Do you need us to hang around while you get in the house?"

"No. I'll be fine. Thank you again, Constables. Your intervention is much appreciated."

"Very well, and you're welcome. Don't be afraid to give us a call, always willing to help out a fellow officer. Have a good evening, ma'am."

"Thank you." After the officers left, Sam collected the plant from the passenger seat and stopped off at Doreen's. "A present for all you do. Thanks so much for calling the police, Doreen. I wasn't sure how that was going to pan out. Chris was far angrier than normal."

"You shouldn't have. It's beautiful. Come in, dear."

They walked into the lounge. Doreen placed the plant on the small table, at the same time Sonny came to greet Sam.

"I had grave concerns about that myself," Doreen said. "Once I saw you refusing to get out of the car, I just knew things weren't going right out there. You didn't mind me ringing the police, did you?"

"Not at all. Serves him right for showing up out of the blue like that."

"He'd been sat out there for a good hour. I was observing him on and off. He was making me anxious. He lashed out at his steering wheel a few times, so I knew he was getting wound up."

"You're a smart lady. I'm so lucky to have you on my side. Not only do you look after Sonny during the day for me but you're my guardian angel when things appear to be wrong, as well. I truly can't thank you enough."

Doreen smiled. "Stop it now. I'm doing nothing out of the ordinary, I'm just helping a valuable friend out, that's all."

"You do so much more than that, without even realising it. How has the boy been today?" Sam ruffled the fluffy mop on Sonny's head, and her hand sank through his soft fur. He moaned and jumped up. She bent down to say hello, and he licked her face.

"Soppy as ever. He really is a dream to look after."

"Right, between us, we've taken up enough of your time today. I'd love to take you out for a meal soon, to really show how grateful I am to have you in my life, Doreen."

She flapped her hand. "Oh no, that would mean me having to dress up. Those days have gone for me, dear. You keep your money in your pocket. Sonny is a welcome distraction to me and stops me from getting lonely, so we're both doing each other a favour at the end of the day."

"If you're sure. Is there anything you need help with around the house? Maybe I can get something fixed for you as repayment."

Doreen shook her head. "Don't be silly. Now be off with you, I'm sure you've got better things to do than spend all your time hanging around here, arguing with me."

"I'm not going to win, am I?"

Doreen smiled and touched her arm. "I'll see you out. Sonny's bag is waiting in the hallway. I've washed his dish, so there's no need for you to do that again."

Sam followed her neighbour into the hallway. "Whatever did I do to deserve a friend like you?"

"Get away with you. Enjoy your evening. Don't be afraid to call out if Chris shows up again."

"I don't think that's likely to happen, but thank you."

Sam and Sonny went back to the house long enough for Sam to deposit his bag of goodies and change into her flat shoes, then they set off on their evening walk. A cool breeze had picked up, and she pulled her jacket around herself as they entered the park. She let Sonny off his lead. He ran to the nearest tree and sniffed the latest squirrel's scent around its base.

She kept her mind busy, going through the notes she needed to make when she returned home instead of reliving the contretemps she'd had with Chris. She called Sonny to heel twenty minutes later, and they began their walk back to the house.

After feeding Sonny his dinner, Sam popped a couple of slices of bread in the toaster and opened a can of baked beans. The dinner of queens, or not as the case may be. It was all she felt like eating until she realised she'd already eaten her quota of carbs for the day at lunchtime in the shape of the sandwich. *What the heck, one day won't matter. I'll cut back tomorrow and take a salad to work for lunch.* She laughed, knowing the probability of that coming to fruition was zero.

She received two phone calls, both of which interrupted her flow of concentration. The first was from her sister, calling back true to her word. Thankfully, the call was brief, just a quick check on how she was, and then ten minutes later Rhys rang.

"I was just thinking about you," she fibbed, knee-deep in notes.

"You were? I thought you'd be snowed under by what you told me earlier."

"I was. I've finished now." She crossed her fingers to combat the lie she had just told. "How was work today?"

"Hectic. I didn't even stop for lunch so I'm starving. I guess a takeaway for one is on the agenda for this evening. Have you eaten?"

"Umm... yes, sort of."

"Meaning?"

"I had beans on toast. I enjoyed it, it made a change."

"Hmm... it's hardly a satisfying meal after a long day at

work. That's it, nagging over now. We could always go out for a nice pub meal tomorrow evening, my treat."

"We'll see how things go tomorrow, eh?"

"I'll leave it with you. Well, I'm going to get my dinner sorted then take Benji for a quick walk."

"I'll call you during the day. It's unfortunate my team are on shift this weekend." She sighed. "Oh well, never mind."

"We'll just have to make up for it tomorrow evening. Would it be all right if I stayed over?"

"Of course. I'd be offended if you didn't."

CHAPTER 4

*A*fter an exceptionally restless night, Sam showered and got ready for work. She took Sonny for his morning walk, dropped him off at Doreen's and then drove to work. As promised, she arrived half an hour early. She poured herself a cup of coffee that she had missed out on at home and continued making her notes before the other members of the team showed up.

Bob knocked on her door and poked his head into the room. "You're early. I missed you giving me a hand getting out of the car this morning," he quipped.

"Shit happens, eh, partner?" She grinned and shooed him out of the room, aware that she had thirty minutes to finish off her task in hand. Sam emerged from the office twenty minutes later. "Morning, all. Plod on with what you were doing yesterday. I'm about to head downstairs to hold the conference—not ideal being held on a Saturday, but needs must. I doubt if the bulletin will go out until this evening. Jesus, why did I agree to hold it today? I must be nuts. And I'll thank you not to comment on the last part." She glared at her partner who had opened his mouth to speak.

Bob pulled an imaginary zip across his lips and then smirked. "Do you need any company down there or will you be all right in the shark-infested waters by yourself?"

"Christ, as if I wasn't concerned enough you have to throw a remark like that into the ring."

He grinned. "Sorry."

"No, you're not. Don't lie. I'll see you later, if I survive the mauling."

The team shouted good luck in unison as she left the main office and descended the stairs on heavy, reluctant legs, taking the file, containing her notes and the images of the suspects and the victims, with her. Jackie was waiting for her in the room off the conference room.

"Hey, you look like death warmed up, are you sure you're up to this?"

"Blimey, don't say that. Maybe I should have worn some makeup today. Damn, I knew I'd forget something in my haste to get to work early."

Jackie smiled and dug into her handbag. She withdrew some eyeshadow and blusher and proceeded to dab it on in the appropriate places on Sam's pale face. "There you are, at least you have some colour in your cheeks now."

"You're amazing. Is it filling up in there?"

Jackie poked her head into the room. "Yep. Which has surprised me. I thought we were chancing our arm calling in a favour from the press on a Saturday."

"Yeah, I had the same sinking feeling upstairs." Sam inhaled and exhaled a few calming breaths. Her heart rate lowered enough for her to tell Jackie that she was ready. "Bloody gets me every time. I should be used to these by now. Does it ever get any easier?"

"Most officers feel the same way to begin with. You'll be fine once you're up there and in your stride. I won't say the obvious, imagine them all naked, because I've seen what's out there, and it ain't pretty."

Sam laughed. "You're a scream. Let's crack on and get this out of the way before my nerves get the better of me again."

She followed Jackie onto the stage that had been set up, draped in the constabulary's emblem, and they sat. Jackie made the introductions. Sam recognised a few of the journalists in attendance and smiled at a couple of them.

"I'll hand you over to DI Sam Cobbs now."

The camera rolling at the front did its very best to distract Sam, but she dug in and came up with the goods.

"So, to sum up, we have a van that we need to identify. Have you seen this van in the vicinity in the last week? If so, call the number at the bottom of your screens now. Likewise, if you've seen any of the people in the photographs in the past week, do the right thing, let us know. One of the women involved in this possible abduction case has diabetes, and her parents are naturally very concerned about what will happen to her if the correct medication isn't administered at the appropriate time. Please, avoid having that on your conscience, contact us today and let us know when and where you saw these individuals and we'll do the rest. It's imperative that we find these people, and quickly. One last thing before I open up the floor for questions. I can't emphasise enough how important it is for hikers out on the fells to remain vigilant. We have two couples reported missing already this week. Please take care, we don't want anyone else going missing in the near future. If you're in doubt about anyone approaching you, make a scene, do your very best to gain someone's attention and remain safe. My advice would be to trust no one. As you can see from the photo, this couple appear to set out to befriend their targets. To me, they have an agenda. Be aware of your surroundings at all times."

Jackie took her cue from Sam. "Any questions, we have a few minutes spare?" Jackie asked the journalists.

"Yes, I have one." Clive Carter, an aggressive journalist from the local paper, raised his hand.

"Go ahead, Mr Carter," Sam replied, her stomach clenching into a tight knot when their gazes met.

"How do we know these couples haven't just taken off elsewhere?"

"Fair point. I should have filled you in. Both cars belonging to the missing couples have been found, one burnt out and the other abandoned in a car park in Grasmere, close to the pub where these images were obtained."

"Have there been any other attempts at abduction?" Carter asked.

"Not that we are aware of. That's the reason I've called the conference today. Maybe someone else has been approached by this couple in recent weeks." Sam held up the photo again and pointed to the possible suspects. "Do you recognise them? If anyone else has spoken to them in the past, please come forward, ring me on the number at the bottom of your screen."

"Any other questions?" Jackie asked.

A few of the other journalists raised their hands and asked inept questions, and then the room fell quiet, so Jackie brought the conference to a close and thanked the crowd for attending, especially on a Saturday. Sam left the stage and swept past Clive Carter. The man tapped her on the shoulder.

"Mr Carter, was there something you forgot to ask?"

"A word in your shell-like, if you have the time, Inspector."

Sam frowned. "About what?"

He bared his teeth in what could only be described as an awkward smile. "It's personal."

Sam inclined her head and repeated the word, "Personal? Okay, why don't we go next door, out of earshot of the others?"

He nodded, and Sam led the way. Once the door was shut behind them, he stood in front of her, shuffling from one foot to the other. She'd never seen him acting so insecurely before. He'd always been the bane of her life, the absolute pain in her derrière, virtually since the day they had met.

Sam folded her arms and tapped her foot. "Come on, spit it out. What's bothering you, Mr Carter?"

"My sister has had a problem with her fella, and I'm worried the situation is going to get out of hand. I'm aware of the statistics concerning attacks, assaults and even murders against women. I'm determined not to allow her to become just a number. I thought I'd have a word with you on the quiet, see if you wouldn't mind offering me some advice on how to go about getting him to back off without it backfiring."

"Is that so? Well, first, I have to say I admire your balls for seeking out my advice, it's not like we're best pals, are we?"

"Ouch! Which is why I hesitated in burdening you with this in the first place." He turned to walk away, but Sam clutched his arm.

"Not so fast. Unlike some of my colleagues, I'm not one for bearing a grudge. You're going to need to give me more details."

"Thank you. I know I can be the utter bastard in the pack occasionally, however, I have to tell you that I admire your steely grit and determination to get the job done."

"Answer me this, if you will? Do you give my male counterparts an equally tough time? Or do you save all your pent-up anger and only aim it in my direction?"

"That's harsh, I'm not that bad."

"Really? It depends if you're on the receiving end or not."

He had the decency to drop his head in shame and mumble a low apology.

"So you should be. Come up to my office with me, and I'll take down the necessary details. I won't even ask for anything in exchange." She winked and turned on her heel.

Jackie entered the room. "Is everything all right? You shouldn't be in here, Mr Carter. The inspector is a very busy person and needs to get on."

"I know that. She's agreed to follow up on something personal for me."

"Oh, I see." Jackie looked at Sam for guidance.

"It's fine. Thanks for organising the conference, Jackie. I'll let you know if anything comes of it at the start of next week."

"If you wouldn't mind. I'm off for the weekend now."

"Sorry to have put you out. Enjoy the rest of your weekend."

"You didn't. See you Monday, don't work too hard." Jackie pointed at Carter and said, "And don't go giving the inspector any unnecessary hassle, especially if she's doing you a favour, you hear me?"

His flattened hand hit his chest. "I wouldn't dream of it. I think the inspector and I have a new understanding, don't we, DI Cobbs?"

"I'm not sure I'd go as far as to say that just yet, Mr Carter." Sam took a few paces, expecting Carter to follow her up the concrete steps to the incident room. She entered the room and swiftly moved towards the whiteboard which she swivelled in the opposite direction, away from prying eyes.

"Everyone, this is Clive Carter from the local rag. We'll be in my office for the next ten minutes or so. The conference went well. It's a waiting game now. I'm not sure when the TV bulletin will be aired, being a Saturday."

"I can help with that, it's usually at around one and then repeated sometime around six-fifteen," Carter replied.

"Great, better than I was expecting. Can I get you a coffee?"

"White with two sugars, thanks."

Sam fixed them both a coffee and glanced in her partner's direction. Bob was staring at her aghast, shaking his head. She had to suppress the giggle threatening to erupt, aware of what must be running through his confused mind. Drinks made, she pushed open the door to the office with her foot and invited Carter to join her. "Take a seat."

"I have to say, I expected a swankier office than this."

She laughed. "Maybe you should lower your expectations where the Cumbria Constabulary is concerned, Mr Carter."

"Already done, Inspector." He noticed the view on the way to his seat. "At least you have great scenery to while away your day."

"You think I have time to gaze out of my window all day, is that what you're implying?"

He cringed. "I knew it would come out wrong. No, that's not what I was inferring at all. Shall we start again?"

"Why not? How can I help today, Mr Carter?" Sam slid a sheet of paper and a pen in front of her ready to jot down any relevant information.

"My sister's name is Tamzin Carter. She was seeing David Warren for a couple of months. Everything started off great, but then he started popping up outside her work."

"Where does she work?"

"At the local builders' merchants. As soon as she told me, alarm bells started ringing. Enough for me to want to check out what he was up to myself."

Sam's eyebrow shot up. "That was brave of you."

He laughed. "Not really. I stayed in my car, parked discreetly and observed his movements when he showed up.

I couldn't believe what I bloody saw. He even had a pair of binoculars to hand. Anyway, the more I watched him, watching her, the more my insides knotted. His face contorted with rage every time she spoke to a bloke in the yard, be it a customer or one of her colleagues. I was so shocked it rattled me to think of her being alone with him. I picked her up from work that evening and took her to the pub, sat her down and asked if there was anything wrong. That's when the tears came. Once the tap opened, it refused to stop. It was embarrassing, everyone else in the pub staring at us like that."

Sam inclined her head and frowned.

"Hear me out before you judge what I'm saying," he said.

Sam nodded, and he continued.

"After she'd finally calmed down a bit, she informed me that David had started hitting her if she answered him back. I was fuming, I told her to do the right thing and end the relationship. She said she couldn't do that because…"

"Because?"

"He'd threatened her that he would come after her family and cause them harm."

Sam tutted. "Sounds a bit of a psycho to me, you did the right thing bringing this to my attention. When did this happen?"

"Last week. I've been keeping an eye on my sis ever since but then I'm not the only one. He's been there, following her, stalking her, if you like. When she went out for the evening with her friends, he was skulking in the bar, hidden behind a pillar. She didn't notice him, but I did. I watched the anger surface, and Tamzin was only sat there drinking with her girlfriends. No other men spoke to them during the evening, and yet his anger increased more and more. It sickened me. Something has to be done about this moron. I was wondering if you might be able to check the system for me, you know, see if he has a record for this type of thing."

"You're going to need to file a complaint first. That's how these things work, I'm afraid. We can't just delve into someone's background willy-nilly, there has to be reasonable doubt to begin with."

He tilted his head. "Is that right?" His expression was one of disbelief.

"Let me check, see what I can find out. If there's anything, then your sister needs to file a complaint before we take matters further. I'm sorry, I'm not prepared to put my career on the line over this issue."

"I understand."

He gave her David Warren's address. "I'll be right back."

She left her office and made a beeline towards Claire. "I need you to look up someone for me, Claire, see if they're in the system."

"Of course, boss. What's the name?"

"David Warren. He lives at forty Forrest Road, Workington."

"What's going on?" Bob called over. "Why is he here, hounding you?"

"He's not *hounding* me. I'll fill you in later." Sam turned her back on him.

"Ah, here we are. Ouch, he's a nasty piece of work. Harassment charges from three different women. One charge of sexual assault, but the charge was later dropped by his accuser."

"Bugger. Okay, that's good enough for me. Thanks, Claire."

Armed with the new information, Sam returned to the office and sat opposite Carter. "You were right to be concerned. I suggest you bring your sister into the station to make a complaint pretty sharpish."

"Now you're worrying me. Can't you tell me more?"

"Sorry, not if I value my job. Just do as I've suggested, and quickly. Is there anything else I can do for you?"

"No. You've done more than enough. Thank you, Inspector, I appreciate you going out on a limb for me."

He downed the rest of his drink, and Sam showed him back downstairs where he shook her hand.

"If ever you need an extra hand anytime, ring me." He gave her one of his business cards.

"I'll try to remember that. I hope things turn out for the best with your sister. Let me know, if you would."

"I will. Thanks for seeing me."

Sam rejoined the others in the incident room and briefly filled them in.

"Seriously? That guy has got some nerve coming here after the way he's treated you in the past."

"Desperate people end up taking desperate measures, you know that, Bob. I was happy to help if it means keeping another woman safe."

"I agree," Claire said. "The guy sounds a bloody creep, judging by his record. He had a right to be concerned."

Sam smiled. "We sisters need to look out for each other. Let's face it, no other bugger is going to do it for us, are they?"

"What bollocks that is," Bob shouted.

Sam's gaze rose to the ceiling, and Claire shook her head.

"Get a life, Bob," Claire said. "You men have no idea what women go through. Most of the time you're oblivious to how other men treat us. At the end of the day, we have every right to be here as any of our male counterparts. Some men find that hard to accept, shame on them. Maybe they feel threatened, maybe it's about them thinking they're the more dominant gender, who knows? It has to stop, though. We're equals, and men need to start treating us as such."

Sam and Suzanna applauded Claire's speech.

"I couldn't have said it better myself, Claire," Sam replied.

Bob sighed. "Yeah, I know all that, but not all men are the same."

Sam shrugged. "Did we say they are? We know it's a minority we're dealing with, although after hearing some reports on the news about what state the Met Police is in… yeah, let's not go there. I'm warning you now, if ever I hear any misogynistic remarks come from any of you guys, it'll be the last thing you ever say or do on this team. There is no distinction between the genders, let's all remember that going forward."

Every male in the room nodded and looked sheepish.

"Good. Lecture over. I run a happy ship, you're all aware of that. Let's keep the momentum going with the investigation and hope that something comes of the conference being aired later on. As you were. I have paperwork of my own to attend to."

CHAPTER 5

"I took them their food, and she's sick. I don't like the look of her, Vic."

He glared at April from the sofa. "What do you want me to do about it?"

"We need to discuss this. Her fella says if she doesn't get insulin soon, she could go into a coma or even die. What then?"

"Don't hassle me, woman. Deal with it yourself. I want no part of it."

"What? How can I deal with this alone? You're not listening to me, she needs either to go to hospital or at the very least to see a doctor."

"It ain't happening. So stop your nagging. Do what's expected of you, feed and water them and leave them to it."

Furious, she launched herself at him and screamed, "I didn't sign up for this. She's ill. You haven't seen her, she's going to bloody die. I don't, no, I won't, have her death on my conscience."

He clamped a hand around her wrist. "Don't fly off the

handle at me. You've got one job to do, to feed them, it's me who takes all the risks around here."

"Bollocks. I've had it. You can drop me into town and leave me to find my own way home."

"Don't talk shite. I'm not leaving here and neither are you. You were aware of the risks when you signed up for this."

"Well, I'm telling you now, I've had enough. I want out. I couldn't live with myself if she, or any of the others, die."

He stared thunderously at her, lost for words for an instant, and then, as his temper flared, he lashed out and gave her a good hiding. He held a hand over her mouth to muffle her pleading for him to stop. She was beneath him now, cowering from his clenched fists.

"Vic, stop it. You're hurting me."

"Good, that was my intention. Challenge me, would you? Why? What good is it going to do you in the end?"

"I'm sorry. Let me go, Vic."

He pushed her away from him and switched the TV on. "Get out of my sight."

April hobbled out of the small lounge and went back into the kitchen. She finished preparing the sandwiches for their other captives and made them each a cup of coffee. She took the tray upstairs and unlocked the first door. Two petrified faces stared at her from the bed. They were both bound by the feet, and their hands were tied behind their backs.

"Food is here."

"Please, why are you doing this to us?" Michelle asked, her voice trembling with fear. "What have we ever done to you? I thought we were friends."

"Shut up. I've had it up to here with your whining. Eat your lunch and keep quiet."

"How are we supposed to eat with our hands tied? You bring us food and drink, expecting us to be able to feed ourselves, and yet…"

April conceded the truth behind her words. She loosened Michelle's hands. "I'll untie one of you. Any smart moves, I've got a knife, I'll slit your throats in an instant. Don't push me, Michelle."

"I won't, I promise. Thank you, we're grateful for small mercies. How long are you going to keep us here?"

"For as long as it takes. Now eat. You'll have to feed him. I'll tie you up again when I collect your cups and plates. Don't try anything foolish." She backed out of the room and went next door to check on Lorna and James, even though something had made her look in on the couple ten minutes earlier.

"Please. We need medical assistance for her," James pleaded, tears staining his cheeks.

Lorna was unconscious on the bed, her hands tied behind her. "I'm going to put the tray down and untie you. Wake her up and get some food into her, maybe that will help."

He shook his head. "I'm telling you, it won't. She's going to die if she doesn't get to a doctor soon."

"It's the best I can offer at the moment. I've tried to plead your case, but he's not accepting it. I'll help you feed her. She needs to keep her blood sugar up, isn't that how it works?" April asked, unsure what she was talking about. She untied James's hands and backed up a few paces. "Don't try anything, I have a knife and I'm not afraid to use it."

"I won't. My only concern lies with Lorna."

"Help me to sit her up." April tugged at Lorna's right arm, and James reached for the young woman's left one. Between them they sat her upright against the wall. Her head lolled over towards James. She was out of it. Tugging her into place had no impact on her unconscious state.

James touched April's hand and begged, "You have to help us get out of here. She doesn't deserve to die in this hellhole.

I can see you're a compassionate person. This is all down to him, isn't it? You don't really want to be involved, do you?"

April backed away from the bed. "You don't know what you're talking about. We're in this together. Stop hassling me. Let's feed her, she has to be our priority, not your selfish pleas to be set free."

"Selfish? If you think that's being selfish then there's no hope. I'm prepared to do anything for Lorna, anything. Have you got that?"

She drifted forward again. "Feed her and keep your mouth shut. I've heard enough of your trash for one day."

He reached for her hand.

She jumped back and removed the knife from the pocket of her jeans and pointed it at him. "I'm warning you. Don't underestimate my capabilities, arsehole. Feed her."

"I can't force-feed her. Don't be so ridiculous. You might as well kill us both now, at least our deaths will be over with. Leave her in this state, and all her organs are going to start shutting down. Are you prepared for that?"

"What's going on here?" Vic's angry voice made her jump. "Why is he untied? Bloody woman, you can't even get that right."

"Vic, don't shout at me. How else are they going to feed themselves?"

His glare cut through her like a jagged shard of glass.

"Have you untied the others?"

"Only the girl. Don't worry, I have it in hand."

A door squeaked on the landing. He growled and bolted out of the room. "Where the fuck do you think you're going? Come back here, bitch."

April shuddered when Michelle's scream filled the cottage. April kept her gaze focussed on James tearing into his sandwich.

Several grunts and whacks came from the landing, and then a door slammed. More shouting erupted in the room next door, and then silence.

April's body quaked with fear. She'd screwed up and knew he would punish her next. "Eat it quickly, I have to tie you up again before he comes back."

"You don't have to do anything. Stand up for yourself, for *us*, don't let him get away with this, please."

April panicked when she heard the door open on the landing again. Vic's heavy footsteps came towards the door.

The next thing she knew, his fist was connecting with her jaw, the force knocking her to the floor. He stormed across the room and tied James's hands.

"Why are you keeping us here? Lorna needs medical help, she's going to be no good to you dead, is she?"

"Listen up, shithead. Neither of you is indispensable, so stop whining. If she dies, I'll kill you as well and go on the hunt for another couple to fill your shoes, it's as simple as that." With James now secured, he dragged April to her feet and pushed her out of the room, locking the door behind him. "Get downstairs. You ever untie them again, and they won't be the only ones I'll be burying in the back garden, you hear me?"

"Yes. How else am I supposed to feed them all?"

"Doh, with your own hands. If God gave you brains when you were born, fuck knows where they've bloody gone since. You're getting on my tits. In there, I've got something to tell you." He shoved her into the lounge. There was horse racing on the TV. "You've made me miss the first race now." He thumped her in the stomach, and she crashed onto the sofa. "Enough about the racing. While you were upstairs, fucking it up, the news came on, and guess what?"

April stared at him and shrugged.

128

"Go on, guess." He was acting like an excited child, his face lit up displaying a toothy grin.

"I can't guess."

"You're no fun any more. You used to be when we first met, not these days."

"I'm sorry. Tell me."

"We were all over the news bulletin."

She scrambled to sit upright, her pulse racing. "What? They know who we are, and you're standing there, grinning about it?"

"Idiot. It's the thrill of the experience, outwitting the useless boys in blue, or in this case, girl in blue. They've got a fit bird in charge of the case. And when I say fit, I mean *really* fit. Even though she's the filth, I definitely wouldn't mind copping a feel with that copper." He laughed at his own poor joke.

"Are you crazy? What did they say about us?"

"That they're requesting to speak with us and warning others not to come near us. They showed a video of us with the last couple we picked up."

"Fuck." She ran a hand through her messed-up hair. "And you think that's funny? You're even more warped than I've given you credit for. What else did they say?"

"Yeah, it's fun. I get a thrill out of shitting around with the cops. They told people to take care and to be vigilant in the area."

"Well, that's scuppered any plans you had to kidnap anyone else then, hasn't it?"

"Has it fuck! Nope, we're going to have to think on our feet, that's all. Although they do know we have a black van, so we might need to alter that before we strike again."

Her breathing suddenly came in short, sharp bursts, and her head throbbed as though it was about to explode.

"What's wrong with you?" he demanded, getting in her face.

She pushed him away and clawed at her chest. "I can't breathe. I'm having a panic attack."

He paced the floor. "Fuck, you're an utter waste of space. What do you expect me to do about it?"

"Paper bag. I need... a paper... bag."

He held his arms out to the sides. "What am I? A bloody miracle worker? Like we have one of those lying around. Everything is plastic. What else?"

April stood and staggered into the hallway; he was stressing her out too much. She knew how to combat the attack but without the added grief. She leaned against the wall and focussed on one thing, breathing deeply in and out. Slowly, gently, absorbed by that one thing she hoped would work. Block out everything else, that's what she needed to do. She was nearly there. She'd managed to get her pulse rate back to normal and her breathing more manageable when he appeared in the hallway and came close to her.

"You all right now?"

"Go away. I need to concentrate."

Vic flung a hand out and growled, "Like I said, you're a fucking waste of space most of the time." He turned and went back into the lounge.

She closed her eyes, hoping to slow her heart rate further still. After another five minutes of performing the intensive calming breathing exercises, she felt much better. She went back into the kitchen and sipped at a glass of water. Her mind racing, trying to source different ways she could get out of this situation. She no longer wanted to be part of a set-up where her partner was revelling being thrust into the limelight. Their faces well known and them being on the wanted list. This wasn't what she'd signed up for when she'd started going out with him. Added to that was the plight of the girl upstairs. She needed a doctor, proper medical treatment, and he couldn't give a shit. She had to get out of there. Maybe when he was asleep that night, maybe that's when she could make her move.

CHAPTER 6

*T*hat evening, at around five, Sam was getting ready to leave when an interesting call came into the incident room. "Boss, I think you need to speak to this lady," Claire said.

"Can you put it through to my office, Claire? Thanks."

Sam shot behind her desk and settled into her chair. She pulled a fresh piece of paper towards her and answered the phone. "Hello, DI Sam Cobbs, how may I help you?"

"I… umm… I know the people on the TV, the ones you're after."

"You do? The man and woman in the black van?"

"Yes."

"Sorry, I didn't catch your name."

"It's Jane Essen."

"Hi, Jane. You sound nervous, please don't be. Just tell me what you know about the couple. In your own time, of course."

"They… they tried to abduct me." The woman sobbed.

She sounded young to Sam. "I'm so sorry. That must have

been a very traumatic experience for you. Can you tell me where and when this occurred?"

"About three weeks ago, my fella and I had just come down from a walk on the fells. We were working our way back to our car. It was within reach of us at the end of the lay-by we had just arrived at, after our long trek."

"Okay. What happened next?"

"This black van stopped beside us. The driver started asking all sorts of questions. Some were off the mark, silly, dumb questions that we couldn't have possibly known the answers to. Don't ask me what they were, I can't remember."

"That doesn't matter. Please go on. You said that you were with your fella?"

"Yes. We've since split up, actually, because of what happened that day."

"That's a shame. What's his name?"

"Kelvin Potter. I can give you his phone number if it will help?"

"Perfect. I'll need to have a chat with him as well."

"Yeah, I didn't think you'd only take my word."

"It's not a case of not believing you, it's more about us gathering all the evidence we can to throw at this couple when we eventually catch up with them."

"I get that." Jane gave Sam her ex's number.

"Thanks for that. You say they tried to abduct you. May I ask how?"

"The man, after asking us nonsensical questions, got out of the van and started pointing out all the fells surrounding us, naming them all and offering us advice on when and how to climb each one. We thought that was nuts. We stood around listening to him for about five minutes then tried to make our excuses to leave. He became agitated. His attention was drawn to the main road running alongside us. We were on the A66 at the time, which is always busy. Anyway, there was a sudden lull in the traffic. Kelvin and I were getting impatient, and we tried to cut him off several times. I think this got his back up. I saw his eyes widen with rage, even though he kept smiling. It made me feel really uncomfortable. I said, 'I'm sorry, we don't wish to appear rude, but we've got to be going now, we have a long journey ahead of us.'"

"And what was the man's reaction to that?"

"It was like a dark cloud descended. He grabbed my arm, I wasn't expecting that, and he tried to force me into the van. The woman got out of the passenger seat and tried to assist him. But Kelvin kicked the man in the balls, and we both ran. Ran faster than we've ever run before. We made it back to Kelvin's car just in time. The van tried to block us in, but Kelvin thought quickly. He reversed onto the grass verge. He put his foot down before the man got the chance to turn the van around and come after us."

"That must have been terrifying for you."

"It was. I had nightmares for a week. Neither of us could talk about anything else. It put our relationship under severe pressure. In the end, I told Kelvin I couldn't see him any more."

"Sorry to hear that. Did you inform the police?"

"No, we spoke about that but we didn't think there was really any point in going to them."

"I can understand. Not wishing to make you feel worse, but sometimes making the police aware of a situation such as this can help to highlight a need for extra patrols in the area."

"Oh gosh, I never thought about it that way. I apologise."

"Don't worry. I don't suppose you managed to get the number of the van, did you?"

"No, we were far too busy doing all we could to get away from them. You don't have time to think when you feel your life is at risk. It just all happened at the speed of a raging tornado, if you get what I mean."

"I do, don't worry. We have forensics on the case, hopefully they'll be able to pick up the number plate from the images we obtained from the CCTV at the pub. How are you now?"

"Seeing the reports on the news has brought it all flooding back to me. My hope was that getting in touch with you might ease the burden. I shuddered when I recognised their faces on TV. Callous bastards, the pair of them. She was as much to blame as he was. She got out of the van with the intention of helping him. How could a woman do that? It's shocking to think people can just pull up alongside another vehicle and try to kidnap someone. Why? Do you know why they're doing this? Have you found or even heard from the other couples they've taken? Are they still alive? Have they killed them?"

Sam sighed. "Our investigation only began at the beginning of the week. Leads have been sparse so far, hence my need to call the press conference today in the hope someone like yourself may come forward. I'm really grateful you had the courage to call me after going through such an ordeal. We haven't got a clue why these couples are being abducted. As far as we're aware, the perpetrators tend to befriend the couples and then make their move."

"Yes, that's what they tried to do to us, but Kelvin and I cottoned on to what they were up to pretty quickly. Maybe they've perfected their skills and learnt from their mistakes of what went wrong when they tried to abduct us. God, it makes me shudder just thinking about it. If we hadn't been alert, they might have got away with it, too. And, I could be dead by now…"

"Sounds like you had your wits about you and got out of the dangerous situation just in time. I'm sorry your relationship has broken down since then. That must be tough on both of you."

"Yes and no. We'd been together about five years, I suppose. Things had become very stale between us anyway, so maybe the relationship had run its course and it was time to move on. It doesn't matter about us. My concern lies with the couples these vile people have abducted. I'm sitting here thinking all sorts. That's why I felt the need to reach out to you."

"I'm so glad you did. I can't thank you enough for plucking up the courage to come forward. If nothing else comes from this phone call, it will give us an insight into how these two are choosing their targets."

"Off the cuff, I think. We did nothing at all to attract their attention, I can assure you."

"Had you noticed the couple before they approached you? Could they have followed you before they made contact, either that day or maybe some other time?"

"No. You think they might have targeted us intentionally, stalked us?"

"At this point, we're unsure what to think. Would you be willing to give us a statement?"

"Yes, I'll do anything to help the investigation. When?"

"I'll get in touch with the desk sergeant now. He'll organise for one of his officers to come out to see you."

"That's fine. I'm here all weekend. I don't tend to go out much these days, not after what happened to us."

"Sorry to hear that. Maybe that will all change once you hear we've caught the perpetrators. Don't let it spoil your enjoyment for life."

"I'll try not to. Thank you for being so understanding, Inspector. Good luck."

"We'll be in touch soon. Thanks for reaching out to me today." Sam ended the call and noted the time on her watch before she rang Kelvin. It was five-fifteen. *One last call and then I'm done for the day.*

"Hello, who is this?"

"Hi, is this Kelvin Potter?"

"It is. Look, if this is a sales call, you can forget it."

"It's not. Please don't hang up. I'm Detective Inspector Sam Cobbs of the Cumbria Constabulary."

"Oh, right. Have I done something wrong?"

"No, not at all. I'm not sure if you've seen the news today. Have you?"

"Is there news on a Saturday? I thought bulletins only went out during the week. What did I miss?"

"I held a press conference regarding an investigation I'm working on."

"Go on. How can I help?"

"I've just been on the phone to your former girlfriend, Jane. She gave me your number."

"Oh, her. Don't tell me she's accused me of something?" His tone had become filled with anger.

"No. There's no need for you to be worried. She saw the news at lunchtime today and got in touch about an incident that occurred a few weeks ago, which involved you both, I gather, just before you broke up."

"Ah, yes, I know the one. It could have turned out to be so much worse if I hadn't had the balls to reverse and get out of there, and what flipping thanks do I get for saving our skins? Yeah, she frigging dumps me."

"Sorry to hear that. In Jane's defence, she was very disturbed by the incident. I could tell she's still struggling at the moment. She doesn't go out much, maybe she's too afraid to admit how scared she is, and what might happen to her if she ventured out again."

"I wasn't aware of that. I ain't gonna feel guilty about it.

She shut down, refused to talk to me. Even dumped me via text message. I thought I meant more to her than that."

"Ouch, she omitted to tell me that part. She gave me her account of what happened that day. Would you mind giving me yours over the phone?"

"Not at all." He went on to tell Sam virtually word for word what Jane had told her about the terrifying episode they had experienced that day. "So lucky to get away, not sure what would have happened to us if they'd succeeded in getting us in that van."

"You were extremely lucky. The news bulletin today showed a picture of the two people in the van. We believe they've likely abducted two couples this week."

"What? Jesus, you don't expect to hear about things going on like this, not around here. Do you know why?"

"Not really, not yet. We intend to find out, though. I know you were terrified during the ordeal but I don't suppose you noted any part of the number plate, did you?"

"No, I didn't even think about that. Our safety and getting the hell out of there was at the forefront of my mind that day. Jane was an absolute mess. When I dropped her home that night, her father wanted to bash the shit out of me, thought I was the reason she was sobbing."

"Again, I'm sorry you had to deal with that. The situation was an untenable one, lots of emotions flying around to deal with."

"You're telling me. I was as shaken up as she was, I can assure you."

"Can you answer me one thing? What do your parents do for a living? I know that sounds a bit strange, but bear with me, if you will?"

"My dad is a carpenter and my mum a nurse in a care home. Why?"

"What about Jane's parents?" She kicked herself for not thinking to ask Jane earlier.

"Umm… her father is a solicitor, and her mother is just a housewife. I know, that's not the right thing to say these days. She's at home all day, how's that?"

Sam laughed. "It'll do. Interesting, thank you. You've been really helpful. I wonder if you wouldn't mind giving us a statement to back up your account of the incident."

"Sure. When?"

"I'll get the desk sergeant to ring you to arrange a time."

"Fine by me. I hope you find these warped fuckers."

"I'm sure we will, thanks to people like you sparing the time to speak to me. Enjoy the rest of your weekend."

"I will. Going to climb Helvellyn tomorrow with a group of friends."

"Crikey, it's been a few years since I attempted that one. I think my legs are still hurting from the trek."

He chortled. "Sounds about right. I've climbed it a few times before. Love to challenge myself. Let's hope it's a clear day, the views are spectacular from the top."

"So I hear. I never quite made it. Maybe one day."

"Force yourself. Go with friends, it'll break the monotony of trying to conquer it on your own."

"Maybe I'll consider going on a work's outing to tackle it." They both laughed, and then Sam said seriously, "I mean it, take care, and try and catch the news later if you can. Also, we're asking all walkers and the residents in the area to remain vigilant at all times."

"That's a given after what we went through."

"I'm glad. Stay safe. Thanks for speaking with me."

"No problem."

Sam replaced the phone in the docking station and returned to the incident room. "Two very interesting phone calls. The gist of which is a couple was approached by the kidnappers around three weeks ago. The male tried to abduct Jane Essen who had just completed a walk on the fells with her then boyfriend—they've since broken up. They were on their way back to the car when a black van pulled up alongside them. The male tried to start a conversation that ended up with him asking some weird questions which alerted the couple that something was wrong. The man tried to abduct Jane and his female associate got out of the van to assist. Her boyfriend kicked the bloke in the nuts, and they managed to get to their vehicle. The boyfriend, Kelvin Potter, then reversed and drove away before the van could follow them."

"Phew! They were damn lucky," Bob said.

"They both believe so, too, even if it cost them their relationship. Has anything else come through as yet?"

"That's a negative. Very disappointing response from the public on this one," Claire replied.

"Okay, we'll get the front desk to handle the calls for the rest of the day. Get your gear together and go home."

Chairs scraped, and computers were switched off en masse. Sam collected her bag from the office, turned off her own computer and then the light and closed the door behind her. "Are you all right, Bob?"

He struggled unsteadily to his feet. "Yep, I'm getting there. Tired, though, after a long week. Could do without having to work this weekend."

Sam nodded. "I was thinking the same in your case. Take tomorrow off, that's an order. In fact, all of you take the day off. I'll cover the phones myself."

Claire gasped. "We can't do that, ma'am, it's not right."

"I'll cover any flack we are likely to get from the chief. Do it. We've worked damn hard all week."

All the team members smiled, said farewell and drifted off. Sam accompanied Bob and rode the lift down to the main entrance. They paused long enough to ask the desk sergeant to monitor any calls that were likely to come into the incident room, and Sam also organised collecting the statements from Jane and Kelvin. Then they left.

"Enjoy your evening, Bob."

"I'll probably fall asleep while I'm eating, I usually do after a long week. Pisses Abigail off, I suppose that's the problem with getting old."

She chuckled. "Old, my arse. You've still got at least forty good years in you yet."

"God, I hope not. If I'm struggling to handle this bloody crutch, I'm not sure how I'm going to cope when my body starts breaking down and refuses to carry me upright."

"You'll cope. This is an inconvenience to you, that's all. Something you weren't prepared for. Have a good one, partner."

"You, too. Are you seeing Rhys this evening?"

She smiled. "I might be."

"Wondered why you were keen to shut up shop early."

She wagged a finger and tutted. "That's not me, and you know it." She opened her door and slipped into the driver's seat.

He did the same, wincing far more than he had all week.

Sam was the first to leave. She rang Rhys the second she hit the main road out of Workington. "I'm on my way home. How are you fixed?"

"The same. Want me to pick up a steak on the way?"

"No, I fancy being lazy this evening. We'll take the dogs for a walk and ring for a takeaway, if that's all right with you?"

"Fine by me. Once in a blue moon can't hurt, can it? How has your day been?"

"Interesting. You?"

"The same. See you soon."

"I'll look forward to it." During the drive home, the investigation, all three couples and their different plights ran through her mind. By the end of the drive, she was more confused than ever about what they were tackling than ever. She pushed the cases aside the second she laid eyes on Rhys getting out of his car. This was her time now.

CHAPTER 7

heir earlier spat forgotten, Vic and April set off on the hunt for yet more victims. They drove around the area for an hour or more, pulling into discreet lay-bys now and then that were shielded by shrubs, aware that the van might stick out to those who may have spotted it on TV at lunchtime.

"Shouldn't we try and get a new vehicle?" April had dared to suggest.

"With what? You know how tight money is. We're fine. I thought about changing it but then figured it's a black van, there are hundreds of them around, and we've done our best to disguise ourselves. You did well there. Good job you had some hair dye hanging around at the cottage and are handy with a pair of scissors."

She glanced at him and smiled. "I do have my uses, occasionally."

He reached out and groped her breast. "Sometimes. Are we all right now?"

She nodded and let out a contented sigh. "I think so, yes."

"Good. I hate it when we fall out. We're better than that."

"Me, too. Can I speak honestly?"

He groaned and rolled his eyes. "Is it going to start another argument?"

"I hope not."

"Let's have it then."

"I'll be glad when all this is over. Once we hand them over to your contact, I want to get our lives back on track."

"I can't argue there. By Monday we should be quids in. We'll hand the couples over and take off for a holiday, how does that sound?"

"Wow! Maybe all this shit has been worth it all along if you're going to whisk me off on holiday. Can we go somewhere exotic?"

"We'll see. Let's get going again. Less chat, more prey hunting."

They both laughed. April switched the radio up a notch, and they sang along to an old Tina Turner song, 'Simply The Best'. Until Vic pointed at a young couple hitching a ride up ahead.

"What if they recognise the van, not us, but the van?" April asked, her stomach tying itself into knots.

"Stop panicking. If they've been out here all day, they won't have seen the news."

"I'll take your word for it."

He squeezed her thigh. "Trust me. I've got this."

The male thumbed the air as they approached.

Vic slowed down and pulled over around twenty feet ahead of them. "Let's give them a warm welcome. Have you got everything prepped in the back?"

"Yep, it's all ready to go in the bag."

"Right. I'll get out and speak with them, and you hop in the back. I'll get the bloke to join me in the front."

"I'm nervous."

"Don't be. There's no reason for it. Just follow my lead. I'll tip you the wink when I think we should make our move."

"I'll be watching."

Vic jumped out of the van, and April climbed in the rear. She lowered the window and listened to the bullshit Vic was telling the couple.

"We'll give you a lift, no problem. Girls in the back, boys up front."

"Are you sure we're not putting you out? Our car is about five miles away."

"We'll be going right past the door, no worries. Make yourselves comfy. I'll bung your bags in the back."

The young blonde got in beside April. "Hi, thanks ever so much for stopping. Dozens of cars have driven past us, and no one has bothered to pull up. I'm Diane."

"Hey, Diane, I'm April. It's no problem for us. Nice day for it, up on the fells."

"Yeah, it was the perfect day. We could see for miles around. I regretted not bringing the tent with us. Sometimes we do that, spend the night up there, beneath the glittering stars."

April smiled. "Sounds like you're a bit of a romantic."

"I am, I mean we are, Stuart is just as bad as me. Isn't nature wonderful? Being out here, exploring all the nooks and crannies and walking the ragged hilltops that nature has formed over the years? It's peaceful and so relaxing. Sorry, I do tend to waffle on."

"You're fine. We're the same. We love travelling around in our van. We've got a tent tucked away in the back, we pitch that here and there when the mood takes us. We live in an extraordinary part of the world that we should appreciate more. I know we complain when we get snowed under in the summer with tourists, but there are times we just need to take it all in and be happy."

"I couldn't agree more."

The van doors at the back slammed, and the front ones opened. Vic and the new bloke jumped in. "This is April." Vic jabbed a thumb over his shoulder.

The young man swivelled in his seat and nodded. "This is cool, you stopping to give us a lift. Thanks, it's good to meet you, April. I'm Stuart."

"Likewise, Stuart. Anything to help out fellow nature lovers. I've been having a chat here with Diane."

"Typical women. Always keen to have a natter, isn't that right, love?" Vic shouted and winked at her in the rear-view mirror.

"Life is a merry-go-round, we're here to enjoy it. Women love to chat, you men need to accept that and get used to it."

"April's right. Women make the world go round, or something like that," Diane said.

Vic tutted. "I see your girlfriend is as bad as mine, always getting her analogies mixed up."

Stuart laughed. "Tell me about it. I've given up correcting her. It becomes wearing after a while. Do you live around here?"

"Not far. We've got a cottage about ten miles away. We're on our way home, so you're not taking us out of our way."

"Good to hear. It's a great area to live in. Do you venture up on the fells much?"

"Now and again, we do. Neither of us has got the energy to do much climbing these days."

"Get on, you're hardly ancient. What are you, about thirty-five?"

Vic nodded. "I am, in a few weeks." He started the engine and indicated into the traffic when a large gap appeared. A car whizzed past them and beeped its horn. The driver was gesticulating furiously out of his window. "Damn idiot. You get some real nutters in these parts during the summer months. Chill mate, all is good."

"Some people find it hard to be mellow, they prefer to live life on the edge and in the fast lane all the time. I've noticed that a lot throughout my career."

"What do you do?"

"I'm a mechanic just like my father before me."

"Ah, it's always good to have a worthwhile trade under your belt, it definitely sets you up in this world."

"My father always says the same thing. What do you do?"

"This and that. I'm in between jobs at the moment. Got made redundant several weeks ago. We've been bumming it around ever since. April keeps telling me I need to get my act together and find another job soon, but..." He leaned towards Stuart and whispered, "I'm enjoying the freedom to be honest with you."

"Carry on doing it until you get bored then. I think that's what would drive me back to work, having to deal with the boredom."

"We don't tend to get bored, do we, love?"

April shook her head. "Never. Too many fab places to go and people to see."

April got back to her conversation with Diane while she kept one eye on Vic, waiting for his prompt. "So you come up here a lot then? Specifically, to this area, or do you travel around?"

Diane looked out of the side window. "Mostly around here, we just love the views, the route feels safe each time we tackle it. Our friends and family think we're nuts, but we do things that come naturally to us, don't we, Stu?"

"Always best to do that."

April spotted Vic wink at her in the mirror and asked, "We were just about to have a bit to eat, fancy some?"

"Tempting, I haven't eaten since I had my porridge this morning. What's on offer?" Diane asked.

"I made some chocolate orange brownies yesterday."

"I'd love one. Stuart, brownies are on offer back here, do you fancy one?"

"I never say no to a brownie."

"What about a drink? We have coffee or blackcurrant cordial, the choice is yours," April said.

"Ooo... I'd love a coffee," Diane replied, her face lighting up. "I think I'm getting withdrawal symptoms from not having my normal quota of caffeine throughout the day."

"Yeah, I'll take a coffee, too, if it's not putting you out," Stuart replied.

"I'll pull in up ahead," Vic said.

April dished out the supplies, and they spent the next ten minutes drinking and eating the luscious brownies she'd made, some of them laced with drugs. It wasn't long before the side effects kicked in. Words began to slur, and the couple's vision blurred.

Diane yawned and apologised. "I guess I'm more tired than I realised, I'm so sorry."

"You're relaxed. Good food, excellent company, and you're unwinding, what's there to complain about?" April patted her hand.

Stuart returned his cup to April. "I could curl up and go to sleep now. It must have been a harder trek today than I realised. The break has been great, and the brownies were delicious."

Vic started the engine. "But you'd still rather get on the road?"

"If that's okay with you, Vic. I hate to bug you after you being so kind and all."

"You're not. We must be making tracks soon, my parents will be wondering where we've got to," Vic lied.

Within seconds, the couple were out cold. Vic reached through the seats, and he and April high-fived each other.

"Another job well done," Vic said.

"We're not home and dry just yet," April reminded him.

"We will be, soon enough. Nice couple. Too trusting, though. Which has been their downfall." He drove up the nearby lane which took them to the cottage.

Together, they dragged the couple through the front door and up the stairs to the box room which contained a single bed and a blanket. There, Vic quickly tied their hands and pushed them on the bed. The movement caused Diane to stir. She lifted her head slightly, smiled at April and promptly fell asleep again.

"She'll be out for the count, they both will until morning now. You'd better check on the others and sort them out some food. Yeah, do that first, get their meals organised. What's on the menu tonight?"

"Will sausages and jacket spud do? It's all I've got left in the fridge until I can get out to the shops."

"Don't stress about it. We'll pick up a few simple provisions in the morning. I love me bangers."

"I know." April left him to finish getting the couple comfortable and paused outside each of the other rooms to have a listen. She heard nothing coming from Michelle and Grant but faint sobs came from the other room, where Lorna and James were. She turned the key in the lock and poked her head around the door. James, still bound, stared at her, wide-eyed.

"What's wrong?" April whispered.

His gaze drifted to Lorna. "She's gone. You've killed her."

Shocked, April backed out of the room and locked the door. She stood there, frozen in time with her hand on the door handle. That's where Vic found her a while later.

149

"Hey, what's going on? I thought I told you to get on with dinner."

"She's dead," April whispered.

"What? Who is?"

"Lorna, I told you she was ill. You've killed her."

His hand darted towards her and gripped her round the throat. "*We* killed her, not just me. We're in this together, got that?"

She nodded, too scared to argue with him, not that she was able to speak anyway.

"We're going to have to get rid of the body." He released her throat.

She coughed and bent over to catch her breath. "We can't. It wouldn't be fair on her family. Can't we dump her by the side of the road somewhere?"

"Are you crazy?" Seconds later, he was on her again, pinning her to the wall. "You want to get us caught, is that your plan?"

She shook her head. Tears bulged and fell onto her cheeks. Annoyed, he let her go, and she dropped to the floor and clutched her throat.

"I'm sorry. I don't think we should bury her, though."

"What else can we do? We can't leave her in the cottage, her body will begin to break down soon, the smell will be horrendous. I have no intention of putting up with that, do you?"

She rubbed her flesh and swallowed several times, trying to ease the pain. "I didn't know that, it's not something I've ever thought about. I'll leave the decision in your hands."

"Like you had an option. Get the shovel out of the shed, and I'll bring the body down."

She stomped down the stairs and peered back over her shoulder when she got to the bottom. The keys of the van were on the table in the hall. She swallowed down the fear almost choking her as much as his hands had moments earlier. *I could go now before he comes down. Do I have it in me? What if he catches me? He'll bury me along with Lorna. I'm so scared, it's affecting my decision-making. What if...?* She strode through the cottage and out into the garden. The shed was unlocked. The shovel was there, leaning against the work-bench. *Maybe I could use it to bash him over the head and release the others. We could all get away from him. Or maybe not. I just don't know what to do for the best. I'm stuck, caught in a huge spider's web like the fly waiting to get swallowed up.*

He shouted her name, startling her. She dropped the shovel. He cursed and ordered, "Bring it here."

April stared down at the young woman's corpse, lying by his feet on the concrete path. Sadness overwhelmed her, freezing her in place.

He strode towards her, his face inches from hers. "You need to get a grip."

"I can't. I'm so scared. You told me no one would die, and here she is... dead."

"So? What, you think this is my fault?"

"No, I'm confused. Sorry, I shouldn't have said that."

"Ah, but it's too late, the words already tumbled out of your mouth. Harsh, unacceptable words. Now what do you think I should do to punish you?"

The whole of her body trembled. "Please, nothing. It was a slip of the tongue. I shouldn't have said anything."

"You're right, you shouldn't. Let's get this over with." He marched to the bottom of the garden and began digging. When he became out of breath from his exertions, he handed the shovel to her. "Your turn."

"What? I can't do much, I haven't got the strength."

He forced the shovel into her hand and sneered. "I've heard enough of your excuses. Now dig until I tell you to stop."

Terrified, she clutched the handle of the tool and stood next to the hole he'd already started digging. She collected half a shovel of soil and added it to the pile.

It turned out that wasn't good enough for him. He clouted her around the head. "Put your back into it. Work up a sweat at something for once in your life or… shall we make this grave big enough for two?"

"I can't do it. No, I won't…"

His fist came from nowhere and crunched against her jaw. She tumbled to the ground, on the edge of the hole. She stared at it, not daring to look up at him in case he belted her again.

He growled and picked up the shovel she had dropped. "You're fucking useless. This is how it's done. Take note, you will be doing your fair share, so get used to the idea."

Her gaze was drawn to the hole, increasing in size. She wondered if he would live up to his threat. Regrets surged through her for not taking the chance to leave when the opportunity was open to her. *I will next time. I have to, or he's going to end up killing me.*

CHAPTER 8

*S*am blew out a breath on Monday morning, weary beyond words after working seven days straight. She was dying for a day off, but that wouldn't be happening until the end of the week. She would need to push through her weariness to stick with her routine today.

The team were all at their desks, waiting for her. "My apologies for running late this morning, one of those days where I wanted to stay in bed."

"With a certain psychiatrist, no doubt." Bob winked.

Sam cringed. "I see your detective skills are way off the mark as usual, DS Jones."

He mumbled an apology and shifted his gaze from hers.

"Accepted. Now, let's recap what we have so far. Where are we with the van?"

Bob cleared his throat. "Alex and I are going over the list we've cobbled together. Looks like we have around twenty vehicles registered at properties close to the relevant areas."

"Okay, that sounds promising. The board is all up to date now with the snippets of information that came our way over the weekend. The conference results were still very disappointing in my opinion. Maybe we'll get further calls today, here's hoping. Let's stick with it. I know how frustrating it is not to have any CCTV footage available for us to sift through, but we need to get past that. I'll be in my office chasing up the service providers about the phones found in the burnt car. Give me a shout if anything comes from your research."

The team all nodded. Sam poured herself a coffee, entered her office and settled behind her desk. She spent the next couple of hours chasing up the phone people, going from one department to another, only to be fobbed off with a promise that someone would return her call within a few hours. Then she went back and forth between answering emails and opening the few brown envelopes lying in her in-tray just to combat the tedium.

Halfway through the long morning, her phone rang. "Hello, DI Sam Cobbs, how may I help you?"

"Yes, please. You're the lady I was hoping to speak to. I saw you on TV over the weekend. I'm desperate for your help. Will you assist me? I know you're probably snowed under with calls but, please, please, you have to help me find my daughter."

"Okay, let's start with you telling me your name first."

"It's Glynis Weaver."

"And what can I do for you, Mrs Weaver?"

"I saw your conference on Saturday. My daughter went hiking on Saturday, and I haven't seen or heard from her since. I'm extremely worried, knowing that there are these awful people in this area, you know... who seem to be... I can't say the word."

"Abducting couples."

Mrs Weaver broke down and cried. "Yes, oh God, please, I don't want this to be true. She's been through hell the last few years after losing her father in a car crash. She's never really got over it, and now she hasn't contacted me over the weekend, or this morning."

"And that's unusual, is it?"

"Yes, we're very close. She only moved in with her boyfriend a few months ago, they've been engaged for around a year and the time was right, but that hasn't stopped her from calling me every day."

"When did you last speak to her?" Sam flipped open her notebook to take notes.

"Around lunchtime on Saturday. She and Stuart were halfway up Fairfield Peak at the time. She said she'd ring me when they were on their way home. I haven't heard from her since. All I keep seeing is your conference going round and round in my head. My fear keeps ebbing and flowing. I'm trying my best to remain calm, but you know what it's like when you get a gut feeling about something."

"I do. Where are you?"

"I'm at home. Sorry, that's not helpful to you. I'm in Little Broughton, out near Cockermouth, do you know it?"

"Yes. I'd like to come and see you in person, if that's all right?"

"Oh my, yes, of course. Maybe that would be better. I'm not one for talking to people on the phone really. I get tongue-tied and nervous. When?"

"I'll leave now and be with you in under half an hour, depending on the traffic, of course. The roads should be pretty clear at this time of the day."

"That would be wonderful. I can't thank you enough for taking me seriously."

"I'll see you soon. Try not to worry too much in the meantime."

"Easier said than done, Inspector."

"What's your full address?"

Mrs Weaver gave her the details, and Sam ended the call.

She gathered the mail she hadn't got around to opening and shoved it back in her in-tray then left her office. She collected a disgruntled Bob on the way.

"What's the rush?" Bob asked on the ride down in the lift.

"A worried mother has just contacted me. She suspects her daughter has gone missing after she went fell-walking on Saturday."

"Shit, not another one. So much for holding a conference, lot of good that's done us."

"Why say that? If I hadn't held one then the woman wouldn't have known to contact me."

"Yeah, I get that, but on the flip side, her daughter couldn't have seen it. Did you tell people to be vigilant?"

"Of course I bloody did. But if she had already set off before the conference had aired, then how is this my fault?"

He tutted. "I didn't say it was your fault per se. It also didn't deter the kidnappers from grabbing someone else either."

Sam shrugged. "If that's what has happened. I need to know the ins and outs first before our minds start working overtime."

"And how is visiting the mother going to do that?"

She pulled a face at him. "Are you intentionally going out of your way to piss me off today?"

The doors squeaked open. Bob patted his chest and said, "Me? I wouldn't dream of it."

She'd had enough of his sarcastic tone to last her the rest of the day. She stormed ahead of him and flew through the main doors without waiting to hold them open for him. He took his time arriving at the car which only incensed her more. She revved the engine in her eagerness to get on the road as he slowly lowered himself into the passenger seat.

"There's no need for you to be so antsy. I have one pace these days, you should know that."

"I do. You shouldn't try winding me up. Belt up," she took pleasure in instructing him.

He stifled a giggle, and she prodded him in the thigh, his good one.

"What was that for?"

She put the car into gear and drove out of the car park and onto the main road. "Stop winding me up. I'm at the end of my tether on this case, and your daft antics aren't helping."

"Antics? What did I do, except struggle to get in the car?"

"All right. Let's call it quits before this escalates into a full-blown argument."

"Never."

Another sarcastic comment. She decided to ignore it and put the radio on instead.

"Can I just point out the obvious?"

"What's that?"

"You haven't entered an address into the satnav, is that wise? You know what your sense of direction is like."

"Cheeky bastard." She clawed at her notebook in her jacket pocket and flung it into his lap. "Last page, you'll find her address. It's out at Little Broughton."

Bob flipped to the page and entered the address into the little screen. "There you go, that'll save us going on a magical mystery tour."

"You can be such a sardonic bastard at times."

He grinned. "I like to keep you on your toes."

"You mean on the edge of a precipice."

"Whatever."

SAM BROUGHT the car to a halt outside a quaint thatched cottage. There were other similar houses dotted in the immediate area, but this one was by far the prettiest. The front garden had lots of shrubs and plants in bloom in a variety of heights and colours. Mrs Weaver was obviously a keen gardener.

"Bloody hell, this would win a gold medal at the Chelsea Flower Show, not that I've ever been there."

Sam laughed. "You took the words out of my mouth. It's stunning. Come on, we have work to do."

Mrs Weaver must have been keeping an eye open for them because she opened the door before either of them had a chance to knock. "Hello. I'm presuming you're Inspector Cobbs?"

"That's right. Pleased to meet you, Mrs Weaver. This is my partner, DS Bob Jones. We were standing here admiring your beautiful garden. It must take up a lot of your time, keeping it looking as pristine as this?"

"It does, but I wouldn't be without it. It's seen me through some very dark days since my husband passed away."

"I'm sure. It's a credit to you, simply stunning."

"Why, thank you. Do come in."

"Would you like us to remove our shoes?" Sam had spotted the cream-coloured carpet in the hallway.

"It's fine, just wipe your feet, that should be sufficient."

Sam did as requested then supported Bob while he wiped his.

"Have you been in a bad accident?" Mrs Weaver asked.

"An argument with a van last month. It's a tad debilitating, nothing I can't handle."

"I can imagine. Come through to the lounge, I'll make us a drink. What do you prefer?"

"Coffee for both of us, thank you," Sam replied. She stepped into the warm lounge. What little sun they had today was streaming through the window. But it was the large inglenook fireplace that caught Sam's eye. Although unlit at this time of year, it was yet another wonderful feature of this gorgeous property. Her envy gene was on full alert. She'd always loved the idea of settling down with a good man in a house like this, a dog lying by the open fire, worn out after a long walk in the surrounding countryside. *One day, girl. Maybe!*

"I can see your mind working overtime," Bob whispered beside her. "Sonny curled up on his bed in front of the fire, you snuggled up on the couch with Rhys."

She shook her head. "Halfway there. I hadn't placed Rhys in the image just yet. Now that you've mentioned it, though, yes, I can see us both sitting there, toasting marshmallows in the fire on a cold winter's day."

Mrs Weaver entered the room carrying a tray holding three cups and a plateful of shortbread biscuits, Sam's favourite. "Here you go. Don't be shy, help yourselves to the biscuits."

"I'd better get in quickly now you've given my partner the go-ahead." Sam smiled, chose the biscuit on the top, collected one of the mugs then took a seat on the sofa. "All right if we sit here?"

"Yes, I prefer the armchair myself. I can't thank you enough for coming out to see me today. I'm going out of my mind with worry, I can tell you." Her gaze drifted to the mantelpiece and the photo of a young couple in a mirrored frame. "She means everything to me."

"Is that Diane? She's very pretty. They seem very happy together."

"Yes, that's my baby. They are so in love. Just like her father and I were when we were their age." She brushed away a tear. "I'm sorry. I think this is harder for me to deal with because I've never really got over her father's death. I feel his presence in every room which is a great source of comfort to me. I just wish he'd been out there, watching over her this weekend. This might never have happened if that were the case."

"Sorry, what is her fiancé's name again?"

"Stuart Ellis. His family lives in the next village. I've tried calling his mother but I think she's away on holiday. I believe it was this week, however, I'm not certain."

"It's okay. We can look into that, I'll grab her details from you before we leave."

Mrs Weaver handed Sam a slip of paper. On it was the name *Kathryn Ellis* and an address. "I know you probably think I'm being foolish getting in touch with you, the trouble is, I was due at the hospital for an appointment with my oncologist this morning, and Diane was supposed to be coming with me. My head is swimming. I've had to cancel my appointment which is only going to push me back further on the list now. Not that I'm complaining, my daughter's safety is paramount in my mind anyway. I don't care what happens to me, if it's my time to go then so be it. Diane has her whole life ahead of her, and I intend to ensure she enjoys every single day of it."

Sam smiled. "I'm sorry to hear about your possible illness. We're going to make this interview as painless as possible for you."

"Thank you. I didn't mean to blurt all of that out. This truly isn't about me, I want to concentrate on what's going on with Diane, not me."

"I can understand what you're saying. I'm going to lay things on the line for you. I'd rather be open with you from the outset."

"Thank you, I'd appreciate that so much, Inspector. It's the not knowing that can often be so destructive to one's mental health, isn't it?"

"I agree. So here's where we are so far. If we're talking about the same perpetrators, we believe they are holding three couples that we're aware of. That figure might be higher, there's no way of knowing if that's the case or not yet."

"Why? Do you know?"

Sam swallowed down the bile that had suddenly filled her throat. "No, the motive isn't clear to us yet. From what we can gather by the video we have obtained, the perpetrators appear to befriend the couples first, to gain their trust, and then... well, that's the part we're unsure about, up until now."

Mrs Weaver sighed and dipped her head. "I need you to be honest with me. Is it possible my daughter might be dead?"

"I can't say that. At this stage, I'm hopeful that isn't the case."

"Have any of the others been found... you know, their bodies?"

"No. Nothing has been discovered so far, which is a fact that we all need to cling on to."

Mrs Weaver nodded. "I see, that's some good news at least."

"Would it be possible for us to have a recent photo of Diane and Stuart?"

Again, Mrs Weaver glanced at the photo on the mantelpiece. "That's the latest I have of them. Do you want it?"

"With your permission, I'd like to take a snap of it with my phone. That should be sufficient."

"Of course. Whatever you need to do is fine by me."

Sam took a photo of the couple and returned to her seat. "Something that has also been highlighted during our investigation which might be of some relevance, is that the other couples have connections in the family who are solicitors. Are you or does Stuart have a family member who is a solicitor?"

"No, no one on our side. I don't believe Stuart has anyone either."

"Okay, like I say, it may just be a coincidence that we're dealing with, nothing concrete as such. Is there anything else you can tell us? What does Diane do for a living?"

"She works in the hospitality industry. She's a wedding planner at one of the large hotels in the area."

"And Stuart?"

"He's an engineer, works for his family's company."

"Interesting. And you say they've been engaged for the past year?"

"Yes, give or take a few months. We had a party at the hotel where Diane works, to celebrate."

"And the wedding is due to take place?"

"Not for a couple of years yet, money is tight for all of us."
So Diane's family isn't wealthy like the others then, but if Stuart's family run a company, do they have money?

"Has Diane mentioned that anyone has been bothering her lately? Or perhaps she's fallen out with someone recently?"

Mrs Weaver looked up and mulled the question over for a few seconds before she responded. "No, or should I say, I don't think so. If she had, she didn't tell me. Excuse my ignorance about police matters and the order in which things take place, but may I ask what you're doing to try and find the couples who went missing last week?"

"It's a pertinent question, and you have a right to ask it. My response is that we're doing our best, as a team. However, the investigation has its drawbacks. For one thing, we haven't, as yet, uncovered any vital evidence or clues that will lead us to the perpetrators."

"Only the video from the pub," Bob added.

"Yes, I meant excluding that. I had hoped putting out a press conference would have been beneficial to the case. To date, we've had very little from the public, which of course is not only disappointing but also very exasperating for me as the Senior Investigating Officer. Without a name for the perpetrators, we're going to struggle to find them. I'm sorry, I'm sure that's not what you want to hear."

Mrs Weaver sighed. "If that's the truth then I'd much rather be aware of it from the beginning. Is there anything I can do to help? I'd willingly come into the station and sit there answering the calls as they come in, if it means getting my daughter back."

"Even if that were allowed, I don't think it would be much use. We're just not getting the volume of calls other conferences have prompted over the years."

"Why do you think that is, Inspector?"

"Perhaps because the news bulletins have been aired over the weekend. I have it on good authority from the press officer that the plea I put out will go out for another few days. Hopefully that will put a different spin on things."

"What about my daughter and Stuart? Will you be able to hold another conference to mention their disappearance? Or do you only hold one conference per investigation?"

"No, not at all. We could hold another one. The only problem with that is we haven't found any further evidence, unlike the last time I sat in front of the press when I had the video footage to show to the public. All we have regarding Diane and Stuart is that they've gone off the radar."

Mrs Weaver's head dropped. "I understand. What are we going to do? I need to get her back, I won't be able to go on without her, not after the death of my husband. If Diane is dead, I might as well kill myself now and get it over with."

Sam swallowed down the lump that was blocking her throat. "Please, don't say that. You're going to have to show some patience. This is the first we've heard about Diane going missing. Don't give up at the first hurdle, I never do, and I don't intend doing it now."

"It was a foolish thing for me to say. Please accept my

apologies, it's just that we're so close, I need her to come home to me."

"No apologies needed. So Diane and Stuart live where?"

"A few streets away, in Chapel Drive, number five."

"I take it you've been to the house to make sure they're not there."

"Umm... no. I thought about it but then decided against it. My daughter never switches her phone off. If she was at home, she would have rung me or at least answered my calls."

"Okay, and you've contacted all their friends? Were they due to meet up with anyone or were they going on the adventure alone?"

"I've tried all the friends I can think of, their closest ones, and no one has heard from them, and yes, they were going alone. Which in itself is unusual, they generally go in a group."

"Why not this time, any idea?"

"I think a few of them had other plans, and Diane and Stuart decided it was either all or nothing, thinking it would be nice if it were just the two of them in the end. I wish to God they hadn't, not after seeing what you had to say during the news bulletin. I know I should be thinking positively about this, but it's extremely difficult given that Diane missed my appointment today. She's usually so reliable, she would never do that. It was the last thing she said to me before we ended our conversation on Saturday, that she had cleared it with her boss and all was okay for her to pick me up and take me to the hospital. She would never let me down, never. Please, you have to believe me. Are you going to help me?"

"Of course we believe you. We're already helping you, we're not in the habit of turning up at someone's house if we aren't taking their claim seriously. We're here and we're going to do all we can to bring Diane and Stuart home safely."

"Thank you."

Sam fished a card out of her jacket pocket and handed it to Mrs Weaver. "Here's my personal number. Please call me day or night if you hear from either of them at all."

"Do you think that's likely? All I have is doubts running through my mind. I hate to be so negative but…"

"I know it must be so difficult for you to think positively right now, but in my experience, if you fail to do it, then it's only going to eat away at you."

Mrs Weaver expelled a large sigh. "I'm sorry, you're right. I'm not usually a negative person, it's just that the last few years haven't been as kind to me, and my confidence is at an all-time low."

"Believe me, I understand that, I truly do. Right, if there's nothing else you can tell us, we're going to shoot off and get our investigation started."

"No, I can't think of anything."

"Would they have travelled in Diane's or Stuart's car?"

"I'm not sure, probably Stuart's."

"Do you happen to know his licence number?"

She shook her head. "I don't, I'm useless remembering them, I don't even know my own, let alone someone else's."

"Don't worry, we can search the system for both vehicles. It's Stuart Ellis, isn't it?"

"Yes, that's right."

"I think we have covered everything now. Maybe you should consider asking a friend to come and sit with you for a few hours, rather than be alone."

"I'll think about it." She stood, and Sam and Bob followed her back into the hallway. "I think I'll have a potter around the garden, it might help take my mind off things."

"Sounds like an excellent idea to me. 'Gardening lightens the darkest of moods' used to be my grandfather's mantra."

"I think he's right. I'll see how I go. It's been nice meeting you. I have confidence in you, Inspector."

Sam smiled and touched Mrs Weaver's forearm. "I promise, we won't let you down. Take care, I'll be in touch soon."

"Thank you. I'll be here, waiting by the phone." She waved as Sam turned to close the gate after them.

Sam opened the passenger door for Bob and then shot around the front of the car and slid behind the steering wheel.

"Nice lady," Bob said.

"Yes, my heart bleeds for her. There's no way her daughter would intentionally let her down, so something has clearly happened to her."

"Yeah, that much is obvious. How the heck are we going to find these people? Three couples and the number is rising, why? And how are the kidnappers getting away with it? Would you trust someone you'd just met? I know I bloody wouldn't."

Sam started the engine and left the tranquil setting. "No, I wouldn't either. Maybe the couples are all guilty of letting their guards down when they're engrossed in their adventures."

"They must do, there's no other reason for it. Only Jane and her fella appear to have had enough sense to suspect something was amiss when the kidnappers tried to speak to them. What are we talking about here, being gullible? Leaving your brains at home when you set off on a climb, when the opposite should be true? Shouldn't you have your wits about you up there on the fells?"

"Yes, you're right, you should. Conversely, I'm surmising the couples were abducted on lower ground, not while they were climbing the mountains."

"Hmm… so when the adrenaline has drifted, you mean."

Sam nodded. "Yes, when the ultimate rush is over and the body is more relaxed."

"That's one explanation for it."

She laughed. "I'm just trying to cast my mind back, working through the emotions of what my own body went through when I last did any climbing."

"Never put myself through the ordeal, so I can't possibly comment."

"Everyone needs to experience an adventure or two in their lives, Bob, while they're still young enough to enjoy it."

"What are you saying? That I'm past it, too old to go on an adventure?"

"If the cap fits, matey. What was Diane's address again?"

"Seven Chapel Drive," Bob said without looking it up in his notebook.

Sam grinned. "I think you'll find it's number five, not seven, feel free to check."

He grumbled under his breath and checked the information. "All right, you win."

"Don't I always?"

"Not all the time, no."

CHAPTER 9

$\mathcal{V}$ic's pacing was driving April nuts. "Why don't you just ring him?"

"I ain't pestering no one. He told me he'd call me Monday morning by ten. He's a couple of hours late."

"Exactly, a genuine mistake has probably been made, the wrong time noted down by one of you."

He stormed across the room and slapped her hard around the face. "Not by me, so don't go flinging your accusations in my direction, woman. Shouldn't you be getting on with lunch?"

"You said we'd go shopping this morning. I've got nothing left for them, or us, to eat."

"Jesus Christ, do I have to do everything around here? Why couldn't you have opened your mouth and said something sooner?"

April turned her head away and mumbled, "I did. God, I didn't want to repeat myself for fear of getting another slap."

"Utter bollocks. I only lay a hand on you when you deserve it. When you ask dumb questions or untie the bods upstairs, don't tell me you didn't deserve it."

She faced him, anger mounting inside. "I didn't. I've always treated you with respect, and yet this is how you bloody treat me."

He took a threatening pace towards her. "And? You want to make something of it? Because I'm in the right frame of mind to dish out some extra punishment. You want some of it?"

"No. Stop it, Vic. Why are you treating me this way? None of this is my fault."

"Don't push me, bitch. What are you saying? That it's my fault our contact hasn't got back to us?"

"It's your fault for not chasing him, yes?" she snapped back, finding the courage for once in her life to stand up for herself. She was sick to death of being his punching bag and living in fear of when the next punch or slap was going to come her way. Things were about to change.

His mouth gaped open, and he took a step back. She could see the cogs churning as he tried to process what she'd done. After a few stressful, silent moments in which she held her breath, not knowing how he was going to react, he nodded.

"Okay, you're right. I shouldn't be taking this shit out on you. I'm sorry, I'll give him a call now." He picked up his mobile and ran a hand through his hair and paced once more.

"Do it! Don't think about it too much, otherwise you'll back out, just do it."

He glanced her way, his eyes full of uncertainty. She'd never seen him in such turmoil before. He scrolled through his phone and held her in his gaze until the call was answered, then he turned his back on her so he could concentrate. "You should have rung me earlier... you what? You can't do that... No way, man, I've got no intention of doing that... What? You contacted me, remember? What do you want from me? They're here, waiting for you... I said you can't do that... we had a deal, I've lived up to my end of the deal, now you need to step up and stump up with the dosh. What the fuck...?" Vic stared at April and held the phone away from him. "He hung up on me."

She ran towards him, and he retreated a few steps.

"What? Why?" she asked, confused.

"He saw us on TV and told me that wasn't part of the deal."

"He what? Shit... what do we do with them now?"

Vic threw himself on the sofa and stared at the clock on the wall ahead of him. "I wish I fucking knew. What the fuck? How could he back out on the deal like this? We're the ones who have put our necks on the line, for what? To be taken for fools. Jesus, this ain't right. We need to cover our costs. I thought I had this deal sewn up nice and tight, and then this shit happens. I'm mortified. This shouldn't be going down this way, it's beyond me how it has come to this. How?"

"All right, calm down. Is there no way back from this, Vic? What if you reduce your fees? Do you think he'll go for that?"

"No. He told me never to contact him again. Said I was unreliable and not worth the hassle. I've never let him down before. I can't believe it has come to this."

"Did you tell him it wasn't our fault we ended up on TV?"

"Of course I fucking did. He couldn't give a toss, said the exposure had damaged the goods we had collected. No one in their right mind would touch them now. That means we're lumbered with them."

"No, there must be a way around this, Vic, don't give up, not now we've come this far."

He hitched up his shoulders and raised his hands. "What do you propose we do then? Because I haven't got a fucking scooby." There was an unopened can of lager on the table next to him. He pulled the tab and downed half the can.

April ran a hand over her face. "We need to put our heads together and come up with a solution."

"I'm done thinking. We should kill them all and move on."

April gasped. "No, we can't do that. You're missing the point, they're a valuable commodity, there must be someone out there willing to take them off our hands. Think, man, think!"

"I've done nothing but think since I ended the call. We're screwed, well and truly."

"What about contacting someone else in the trade. You can do that now you're a free agent, can't you?"

He finished off the rest of the lager and wiped his mouth on the back of his hand. "Nope. He was my only contact, a middle man who kept his cards close to his chest. I have no idea where the others went and I didn't bother asking either. As it stands, he's fucked with us."

"Don't be such a defeatist, there must be a way around this. I refuse to give up, we just can't."

"Tell me what to do then. I'm open to every suggestion you can fling my way."

April sat on the arm of the sofa and placed her head in her hands. "None of this makes any sense. Why? I reckon something else is afoot here and your contact is just making up excuses."

"I tried arguing the toss with him, you heard me, he wasn't interested. We're saddled with them. All we can do is kill them."

"We can't do that. I won't allow it. Why don't we just dump them somewhere, set them free? They won't go blabbing to the cops, not if we threaten their families."

"And what would that solve? Not the money side of things, we'll still be out of pocket. I'm pissed off with this. People have taken me for granted all my bloody life, and it's still happening now."

"Don't get down, love. Between us, we're bound to come up with a solution."

"Are we? I'm out of ideas, my mind is blown, I'm brain dead. I've pinned all my hopes on this deal getting us out of a financial hole, and instead it's got us into more strife. I need to vent my anger and get rid of them."

"No, it's not the answer, Vic. We need to consider what we've got here, how valuable they are."

"What are you saying?" he asked after a slight pause.

She sat up straight and stared at him. "We get in touch with the families."

He frowned. "Why?"

She rolled her eyes to the ceiling. "Think about it. No one else knows the true reason behind us abducting them. Maybe the families will be sitting there, waiting for the call."

"What call? Talk sense, woman."

"Ransom!"

He shot out of his seat and flew at her. She flinched and turned her head away to avoid being struck. He surprised her by planting a hand on either side of her face.

"You beauty. You've struck gold with that idea." He kissed her hard on the lips, taking her breath away.

She smiled, thrilled to be back in his good books. She much preferred this side of him, rather than his inner Mr Hyde, who had showed up far too often lately for her liking.

"See, I knew you could apply yourself when the chips were down. You do have a brain in that pretty little head of yours after all. Yes, we should sit down and draw something up. The last thing we should do is get on the blower and balls things up from the start. Careful consideration needs to be taken before we contact the families."

"I couldn't agree more. I'm going to make us a coffee and get my notebook out. Let's thrash some ideas around, see what solutions we can come up with to our problem."

He kissed her again. "Get your pad, I'll make a start while you make us a drink."

She ran into the kitchen to collect her handbag, which she hooked over her shoulder, and sprinted back into the lounge. "Here you go, I'll be back in a jiffy." She handed him her pretty pink A5 notebook and gold pen which she'd picked up from Poundland at Christmas.

He looked at the items and groaned. "I suppose they'll have to do."

She laughed and skipped into the kitchen. Grateful to have him back onside. This whole exercise had been a stressful one for them both to handle. Hopefully, now that she had come up with a credible idea, maybe things would be a lot better between them. She made the coffee and returned to find him frantically scribbling in the notebook.

"How's it going?" She stood in front of him and held out a mug.

He kept his head down, ignoring the drink until he'd completed the sentence he was writing, then he patted the seat beside him and took the mug, which he placed on the floor by his feet. "Here, feel free to add or alter anything you don't think should be there."

Risky strategy, but she was happy to take a look. "This all seems perfect. You've got a burner phone, haven't you?"

"Yep. All locked away in the van. I'll need to put it on charge for a while. I'll go and get it."

"I'll cast my eye over the rest of your plans."

He kissed her and left the room.

She read through his suggestions, proud that he appeared to have covered every detail that had run through her mind while she'd been making their drinks. He returned, plugged the lead in and sat beside her again.

"Well, what do you think?" he asked.

"Everything looks great to me. I think you've covered all

the bases here. As long as we make the calls from the burner phone there's no way they'll be able to track us down. All we need to consider now is how we get the money from the parents."

"Hmm... I haven't got that far."

She paused to think. "We're going to need to arrange for them to drop off the money at a secure place. Also, we'll have to enforce upon the parents the importance not get in touch with the police. How are we going to do that?"

"Easy, threaten their lives, you know, the young ones we've got upstairs, and if that doesn't work, we could threaten other members of the family, tell them we'll come after them and kill them off, one by one if the police get involved."

"Sounds good to me. We need to work out the finer details. I'll go upstairs, get all the parents' info from them and we can draw up a list of calls to make. Get organised while the phone charges."

"It's going to take a good couple of hours, useless piece of shit, it is. My other phone you can make calls while it's on charge, not this one. Damn shite thing."

"Don't worry. I'd rather take a step back, get everything organised and ready to go first, that way we won't fuck up."

"What would I do without you? We still need to get to the shops to pick up supplies. Maybe we should do that first."

"Makes sense to me."

They hopped in the van and picked up the basic shopping they needed for the next few days. Vic remained in the van, constantly checking his mirrors in case the cops showed up while April filled the basket.

She jumped in the van with two carriers laden with supplies. "Another thirty quid down the drain."

"Bloody hell. I didn't tell you to buy the whole shop."

"I know, I have a lot of mouths to feed, though. I cut corners where I could, Vic, I swear I did."

He revved the engine and pulled away from the shop. "Let's get this shitshow on the road."

CHAPTER 10

*S*am had visited the neighbours on both sides of Diane and Stuart's home. The younger neighbour was really helpful, she had even waved Diane and Stuart off on Saturday afternoon at around three. However, that's where the usefulness had ended.

Now they were on the road, heading back to the station. Bob had already made contact with Claire, given her the information they had about the couple and where they were supposed to be going. It was up to the rest of the team to find something positive for them to investigate.

Thirty minutes later, Sam drew into her allotted space in the station car park. She helped Bob out of the vehicle, and they rode the lift up to the incident room. "Hi, everyone. Any news for us yet?"

Claire smiled and nodded. "Yes, Alex has pulled out all the stops and captured the vehicle on the ANPR camera, heading north."

"Good job, Alex. Can you show me the footage?"

Alex fidgeted in his seat and leaned to one side so Sam could get a better view of the monitor. "This is where I picked them up. They parked their car here. I asked a patrol car to search the location, and yes, they found the vehicle in this car park."

"Great news. Going back to the ANPR, can we make out if anyone is following them?"

"I can have a hunt around, see if I can find anything. It's not something I've been looking for, boss."

She patted his shoulder. "Not a problem. Get on it now and bring me up to date when you can."

"Leave it with me."

"Liam, any news on the van yet?"

"I'm still narrowing things down, boss. Sorry it's taking me so long to get back to you."

"No need to apologise. I'd rather have accurate information to deal with than nothing at all." She glanced around at the team, all of them with their heads down, fervently working on different aspects of the investigation, not that they had gathered much, not really. Nevertheless, she was proud of what they had achieved so far.

AT AROUND FOUR THAT AFTERNOON, Sam kept the pressure up on her team and circled the room again. "Liam, are we any closer to finding out who the van belongs to yet?"

He smiled and waggled his eyebrows. "Maybe. I've whittled it down to five possibilities now. I'm in the process of checking their addresses and where they're situated in relation to where the walkers went missing."

"Can you get the map up and show me? We can work it out together."

The phone rang, and Claire immediately answered it. Sam focussed on the map with Liam but had one ear cocked, listening to Claire's conversation.

"I've put a marker on each of the addresses. What do you think?" Liam asked.

"Will you hold the line a moment?" Claire said.

Sam glanced across the room and inclined her head. "Is that for me?"

"I think you should have a word, yes, boss."

"Sorry, Liam, give me a second to take this call. I'm sensing it could be important." She raced towards Claire's desk and then changed her mind. "Can you put it through to this one for me, Claire?"

The phone rang on the nearby desk, and Sam answered it, "DI Sam Cobbs, how may I help?"

"Not again. Why do I have to keep repeating myself? This is the third time now. You know what, forget it..."

"No, wait. Please don't hang up. You've been put through to the Senior Investigating Officer for the investigation, I'll be the final person you have to speak to, I swear."

The woman on the other end let out a long sigh. "Very well. You people need to understand some of us have our own businesses to run, we haven't got the luxury of spending all day on the phone, not like some folks."

"I appreciate what you're saying and I can only apologise. Can we start over? How about you give me your name?"

"It's Fay Black. I own a little shop, close to Rydal."

Sam brought up the image of the map she'd just been casting an eye over in her mind and nodded. "Okay, I can envisage where you are. How can I help? Do you have some information for us?"

"I believe so, yes. I saw that press conference you put out about the two people in the black van, well, they were in here earlier. Well, she was."

Sam's pulse raced, and her eyes widened. She scrabbled around the desk, searching for a sheet of paper and a pen. "That's great. About what time?"

"This morning, maybe just into the afternoon, I forget now. Something bugged me about the woman when she was in here. There was something familiar about her, but I couldn't quite place her. I know why that is now."

"Why?"

"Because she had dyed her hair since the photo you put out over the weekend. By the time I realised who she was, she'd left the shop. I looked down the road and saw the black van driving off. That's when I put two and two together."

"That's amazing. Have you seen her before? Was the male with her?"

"Yes, she's popped in to do some shopping before only once or twice, I wouldn't call her a regular. Maybe she's staying close by for the holiday season, we get a lot of that around here. Not sure if there was anyone else with her, I got to the window too late to see that, sorry."

"Don't be. What you've told us is a significant help. Would it be possible to send an officer out in the next day or two to take down a statement from you?"

"Yes, as long as they give me some notice. I can ask Shirley to cover the shop for an hour or so while I talk to them."

"Great stuff. Thanks so much for taking the time out of your busy schedule to contact me today. We'll do some digging at our end, see what we can come up with. I don't need to tell you to remain vigilant and out of harm's way, do I?"

"Nope. I've got several deterrents dotted around the shop, don't worry. Maybe I shouldn't have told you that."

Sam chuckled. "I didn't hear a thing. I'll pass on your details, and someone will arrange a meeting with you soon. Thanks again."

"Glad the information was helpful, it's shocking for the residents of this beautiful county of ours to live in fear."

"I couldn't agree more. Take care." Sam ended the call and dashed back to Liam. "What have we got around the Rydal area?"

"Two possibilities. One a cottage up a dirt track, and the other belongs to a farmer here." Liam pointed out the two addresses.

"Hmm... both have potential for holding hostages, away from prying eyes."

"We should get out there before they think about grabbing someone else," Bob suggested.

Sam raised a finger. "While I agree with that notion, we still need to be careful, Bob." She tapped Liam on the shoulder. "Do me a favour, bring up both addresses on Google Earth, let's see the lay of the land before we show up at either location heavy-handed."

Liam worked his magic and brought both locations up on a split screen on his monitor.

"Which one seems most likely to you, Liam?"

"Hard to say, boss. Maybe the farm would be the more likely option, plenty of outbuildings to consider."

"I've got a suggestion," Bob was quick to add.

Sam glanced at him. "Go on. I'm all ears."

"Why don't we put a surveillance vehicle near the cottage and hit the farm mob-handed?"

She mulled over the possibility. "I think you're right, we could do it as a team."

"Umm... dare I say we're going to need backup in the form of an ART as well?"

"Of course. That goes without saying, we have no idea what kind of weapons these guys have or how many of them are involved," Sam agreed.

Bob nodded. "That sounds about right. All we know is that a man and woman are picking the hikers up, but there could be a whole gang of them involved."

"Let's get things organised. I'll ring the ART commander, see how he's fixed and apprise him of the situation." Sam made her way into her office just as the phone rang. "DI Sam Cobbs, how can I help?"

She was greeted by silence.

"Hello, is anyone there?" A slight sob caught Sam's attention. "Please speak to me. There's no need to be scared."

A sniffle and a deep sigh.

"Please, don't be worried about talking to me. Come on, I promise not to bite," she added, hoping to put the person at ease.

"Hello, Inspector. It's me... Vanessa Farrar."

"Mrs Farrar, is everything okay?"

"No... I don't know what to do for the best."

"Why don't you tell me what's wrong, and we'll try and figure out a solution to your problem together?"

Vanessa fell quiet again. "I rang my husband. He warned me not to ring you... but I'm sitting here thinking, just mulling over what might be happening to our little girl, and my heart is breaking for her."

"I know this must be tough on you, Mrs Farrar, we're doing our utmost to bring this investigation to a swift conclusion."

"It's not that... oh God, I shouldn't have rung you, they warned me not to get in touch with the police."

"Wait, who did? The kidnappers? Are you telling me they've been in touch?"

"Yes. No, I truly shouldn't have called. All I'm doing is putting Lorna in yet more danger. I need to go..."

"No, wait. Please, stay on the line. Tell me what's going on. Vanessa? Are you still there?"

The line went dead. Sam flicked through her paperwork and located the woman's phone number and rang her back. At first, she got the engaged tone. Sam rang a second and third time and, eventually, on the fourth time of trying, the distraught woman answered.

"Vanessa, please, you have to tell me what they said."

"I can't. They'll kill her."

"I know there's always a risk but... look, I don't want to raise your hopes, but new evidence has come our way, and we believe we know where the kidnappers are... when I say that, we're dealing with two possible locations within a stone's throw of each other. I'm in the process of organising a raid on the properties."

"My God, no, you can't do that. You're going to put their lives at risk."

Sam covered her eyes with her hand and shook her head. *Their lives are already in danger. We need to make our move and quickly.* "You've come this far, ringing me, you need to tell me what they've said. Vanessa?"

Heavy breathing followed. Sam picked up on the woman's appalling dilemma.

"Money," Vanessa eventually told her. "They've asked us for a large sum of money."

"May I ask how much?"

"A hundred thousand. My husband is trying to secure the funds now."

Shocked, Sam asked, "You're going to pay them?"

"What other option do we have? I know you probably don't agree with what we're doing, but my daughter means everything to us, and she's ill. I just know she is."

"Believe me when I say I totally understand your thought process, but handing over the money won't guarantee getting your daughter back, that rarely happens in cases like this."

"What? That's not what I wanted to hear, Inspector."

"I'm sorry. I shouldn't have blurted it out the way I did. Please forgive me. What else did they say? How are you going to get the money to them?"

Again silence.

"Are you still there, Vanessa?"

"Yes, I'm here. My husband is going to be livid I rang you. The kidnappers warned me not to do it. Told me they would... kill Lorna. No, I'm sorry, I have to go, this was a huge mistake."

"It wasn't. Vanessa, stop. Don't hang up. We can help you. Be there when you make the drop-off."

"No. You can't do that. I won't allow you to put my daughter's life in further jeopardy. We need to do things our way, or the kidnappers' way, without your interference. I'm such an idiot for getting in touch with you. Goodbye, Inspector."

"No... wait," Sam shouted. "Don't go. I can help."

The line went dead, and Sam threw the pen she was holding at the door and screamed. Several worried faces appeared in her doorway.

"Are you all right, boss?" Liam asked.

"I will be when I've had the chance to calm down. Get me a strong coffee, will you?"

"Coming right up."

Bob shooed the others away from the door and entered the room. He lowered himself into the chair opposite. "Are you going to tell me what's going on?"

"They've made a ransom demand, and the Farrars are getting the money together to pay the kidnappers."

"Wow! I wasn't expecting that. Shit, this changes everything."

"I'm bloody aware of that, Bob."

"I was just saying."

"You were stating the obvious, as usual."

He tried to get out of his seat.

"Don't go. I'm sorry for snapping. It's my frustration getting the better of me. Jesus, what a mess."

"It needn't be."

She frowned and asked, "What do you mean by that?"

"We follow the couple to the drop-off point and nab the bastards there."

Sam stretched out her neck and rocked it from side to side. "Possibly, however, if the kidnappers spot us, it's going to put the other hostages at risk."

Bob rubbed his hand across his stubble. "So what's the answer?"

"I'm genuinely not sure about this one. I think I'm going to need to run it past DCI Armstrong, just to cover my back. It's a complex situation."

"That makes sense. I'll leave you to it. I have faith you'll make the right decision, if that helps."

"Thanks, Bob, that means a lot. I'm going to go and see him in person." She left her seat and the office.

Heidi smiled as Sam entered the office. "Sorry to interrupt, is the boss available for a brief chat?"

Heidi checked that his line was free and then rapped on his door. Armstrong bellowed for her to enter.

"Sorry to interrupt, sir. I've got DI Cobbs wanting a word with you, if you can spare her the time."

"Send her in. Thanks, Heidi."

Heidi stood back to let Sam pass. "Can I get either of you a drink?"

Sam held her hand up. "I'm fine, thanks all the same."

"I'll skip one this time round, thanks, Heidi. Take a seat, Sam. You only just caught me, I was getting ready to head home. I have a police award ceremony to attend this evening."

"I wasn't aware there was one, sir, are you up for an award?"

He chortled. "Hardly, no, just one of those functions that everyone has to attend from DCI and higher, more's the pity.

Can't stand the damn occasions myself. I'm sure I could find far better things to do in my spare time."

"Ouch, the joys of being a Chief Inspector, eh? I feel for you, I'd hate to be forced to attend something so boring."

He shrugged. "Enough about my woes, what can I do for you?"

She gave him a quick rundown on the events that had happened in the past week as this was the first time she'd mentioned the investigation to him. He listened attentively with his hands steepled in front of him.

"I see. That is a serious dilemma you find yourself with, Sam, how can I help?"

"By telling me what to do for the best."

He cocked his head to the side. "Why the indecisiveness?"

She blew out a long breath. "I don't know. Maybe at the back of my mind it's because some of the family members are solicitors."

"And you're trying to avoid taking any flack from them if things don't go according to plan, is that it?"

"Maybe. I'm not really sure. Should we go to the two properties or should we follow the Farrars to the drop-off point? Not that Mrs Farrar told me what time or where the exchange was going to take place."

"Go with your gut. Do what you think is right."

"Great, that's no help, sir."

"It's the best I can do." He held his wrist up and peered at his watch. "I'm really going to have to get my skates on."

Sam took the hint to leave. "I understand. I apologise for burdening you with this, sir."

"Nonsense. That's what I'm here for. Why don't you sleep on it overnight, and we'll have a further chat in the morning?"

Jesus, did you just say that? What, and let six people lose their lives when I could have prevented it from happening?

"I'll do that, thanks for the advice, sir. Try to enjoy your evening. I'm sure you will if there's alcohol involved."

"I'm sure I'll cope with that side of things. Go home, get some rest and start again tomorrow with a clear head."

"I will. Thanks, sir."

Deflated by her meeting and lack of support from her senior officer, Sam trudged back to the incident room. Bob raised his head and frowned.

She sighed. "No good. He was on his way out of the door and told me to go home and view the investigation with fresh eyes in the morning."

"Damn. Not the support you were after. What are you going to do now?"

"I'm going to try and call Vanessa Farrar back. I need to find out what we're up against. When and where the drop-off is going to take place, then I'll decide what to do next."

"And if she doesn't tell you?"

"Then we're up shit creek, but I don't want to entertain that thought, not yet." She entered her office, doing her best to ignore the magnificent view that had been the centre of attention during this investigation. Taking several calming breaths, she then took the plunge and picked up the phone. The number rang and rang. Sam was about to hang up when Vanessa's strained voice answered.

"Hello."

"Vanessa, it's Sam Cobbs. Please, don't hang up on me."

"I can't do this, Inspector. We've been over this more times than I care to remember. Goodbye."

"No, Vanessa. I have one question, hear me out, please?" Sam pleaded.

"What is it? Make it quick, my husband is on his way home, and then…"

"Then what? Come on, Vanessa, tell me."

"I can't."

"You're going to meet them, aren't you? The kidnappers." Sam threw a paperweight at the door in the hope of gaining a member of her team's attention.

Liam opened it and stuck his head in the room. "Boss?"

She covered the phone and said, "Get everyone ready, we'll be heading out soon."

He nodded and shut the door.

"Vanessa, don't do this, not alone. Let us be there. Where is the drop-off due to take place, and when?"

"I can't. Oscar would kill me if I told you."

"He won't. You need expert people to handle the exchange. Situations such as this are prone to getting out of hand quickly."

"I... no, I refuse to listen. I have to put my daughter first."

"And you think I'm not? Come on, give me a chance to complete the investigation in a safe, non-disruptive way. If you or your husband meet with the kidnappers without us being there, they could take the money and kill you. What have they got to lose? Is that what you truly want?"

"Of course it isn't. That will never happen."

"Won't it? How much experience do you have in these matters? I'm guessing none."

Vanessa remained silent.

Sam pushed harder, she had to make the obstinate woman see sense. "Let me prove my experience in dealing with people of this ilk. Let me make the exchange."

"What? That's not going to happen. They'll recognise you from the press conference."

"They won't. I'll wear a disguise so I look like you."

"You'd do that... for us?"

"If it means catching these criminals, then yes, I'm prepared to do anything."

"But they'll be expecting both of us to show up, Oscar and me."

"It's okay, we can get around that. We have a member of my team who looks very similar to your husband. All you need to supply is the money. They're bound to want to see it before they let Lorna go."

"I'm not sure. I'm so confused. I don't know what to do for the best. I need to speak with my husband. I know he's going to be furious with me because I've gone behind his back, but what's done is done now."

"That's right. I believe you know that you've done the right thing, contacting me. All I need you to do now is trust me further, to bring this to a satisfactory conclusion." Sam sat back. She'd said all she could say on the matter now, there was nothing else she could add that was likely to change Vanessa's mind.

"All right. I'll tell you."

Sam shot upright again. "That's great to hear. Where and when are you supposed to meet them?"

"Outside the church in Rydal at ten this evening."

"I think I know it. Okay, why don't we arrange to meet up somewhere else at nine-forty-five to make the swap?"

"What about outside Rydal Hall?"

"Yes, that works for me. You've done the right thing, involving me, Vanessa."

"I hope my husband sees it that way. We'll see you later, Inspector."

The line went dead before Sam could say anything further. She rushed out of her office to bring her team up to date. "Guys, it's all kicking off this evening. You'd better inform your loved ones that it's going to be a late one."

"Can you define 'kicking off this evening' for us, boss?" Bob asked, his brow pinched tightly together.

Sam recapped her conversation with Vanessa, emphasising how much she had needed to persuade the woman that she would make the exchange instead of the Farrars.

"Whoa! And she's contacted you behind her husband's back? What the hell is he going to have to say about this... strategy?"

"I'm hoping he'll eventually see sense, admit that Vanessa was in the right and everything will go according to plan. I need to ensure I have the ART onside and lined up to go. The drop-off is due to take place at ten outside the church in Rydal. Liam, do the necessary searches through Google Earth, let's make sure there are enough hiding places in that area for our operation to go ahead smoothly."

"I'll get on it now."

"Alex, you'll be standing in for Bob tonight, as my partner, as you're a similar height and build to Mr Farrar. Oh God, I need to sort out a wig for me so that I look like Vanessa."

"Don't worry, I can sort that for you, boss," Suzanna chipped in. "I'll see what's available in the undercover accessories downstairs."

Sam smiled. "Thanks. You guys are great. Teamwork, that's our forte." She returned to her office and rang the ART commander. She explained the situation to him and asked for his assistance. He agreed to send his best team, including himself, to the location. They were due to meet up at nine-thirty outside Rydal Hall.

Ending the call, Sam took a breather to contemplate what lay ahead of all of them in a few hours. She reached for the phone again and called Rhys; she was going to need his help in pulling this off this evening.

"Hi, I was going to ring you after I'd finished my notes."

"Sorry to disturb you, Rhys. This is an emergency."

"I'm listening. How can I help, Sam? First of all, are you all right?"

"Yes, not that type of emergency. I have to work late this evening, I might not even make it home at all today, it depends on how the exercise works out."

"And you want me to take care of Sonny this evening, is that it?"

"Yes. Ugh… do you mind? I hate to put on you like this. I can call Doreen, ask her if she'll look after him this evening as well as all day."

"I won't hear of it. It's okay. If I have your permission to be in your house while you're not there, that's fine by me."

"Of course you do."

"Then that's sorted. Can you tell me what you'll be up to this evening? Is it a stakeout?"

"A bit more than that. We're hoping to meet up with the kidnappers tonight. They've put in a ransom request to one of the hostages' family. I'm going to do the exchange instead of the mother."

"What? Crap, I wish I hadn't asked now."

Sam laughed. "Maybe I should have held back some of that information. Forget I said anything. In my defence, I will add that all my team will be in attendance along with an ART, so there's really no need for you to be concerned."

"As easy as that, eh? You'll be in my thoughts all evening. Will you ring me once you've completed your mission, if only to prevent me from worrying unnecessarily?"

"It goes without saying. Thanks for being so under-standing about this, Rhys. It makes a difference to have a supportive partner by my side."

"I'll always be that for you, plus a voice of reasoning if ever you want to bounce some ideas off me."

Sam's thoughts flitted back to the letter she had received, and she wondered if now would be the right time to tell him. She swiftly decided it wouldn't be. "It sounds good to hear that, Rhys. Ditto, I'm always here for you as well."

"I know you are. Right, you obviously have a lot to organise before your mission. I wish you oodles of luck, although I'm pretty confident you won't need it."

"Oh no, my team and I need all the luck we can muster on this one. These blasted criminals have proven to be rather elusive up until this point."

"It would be pointless me telling you to be careful, wouldn't it?"

"It would. Look, help yourself to anything you can find in the fridge or the freezer, don't hold back, okay?"

"We'll see. Would there be any point in me preparing something for you?"

"No, none whatsoever. I'll be treating the team to a take-away this evening."

"Sounds like an exceptional plan. You know what they say? An army always marches on its stomach."

She laughed. "No fear of me ever going without food. I rarely skip a meal, no matter what personal trauma I'm having to deal with or how busy I am at work," she said, although it was a bit of a fib, she'd missed plenty of meals lately.

"In all seriousness, a word of caution, if I may? Please don't take any risks out there. I'll be thinking of you."

"Don't worry. I'll have expert people surrounding me at all times. I'll be in touch when I can, and thank you for having my back on this one. I owe you."

"You don't, but I know you're not going to accept that."

Sam ended the call with a smile. Not for the first time, she pinched herself for having him in her life.

CHAPTER 11

"He's inconsolable up there, refusing to eat. I've tried everything to get him to drink as well, but he's having none of it. Reckons he's too upset after seeing his girlfriend die like that," April said.

She had fed the rest of their captives, but James was a law unto himself. She knew Vic wouldn't give a toss. His mind was focussed on one thing, the meeting planned for later. They had held back on calling all the parents to make similar demands. Vic had said it wouldn't make sense and that each drop-off would need to be meticulously organised if they were going to end up rich.

"Don't worry about him. He'll eat when he's ready. We've got bigger fish to fry. I'm going to go out soon, top up the van with diesel, ensure she's running smoothly in case we need to get out of there rapidly."

"Makes sense. My stomach is churning already, and we've got another three hours on the clock to go yet."

He wrapped an arm around her shoulder. "You stress too much, that's your problem."

"One thought I had…" she said hesitantly.

"What's that?"

"Do you think we should have got in touch with one of the other parents first? You know, with Lorna now lying in a grave out back?"

"Nah, I'm willing to take the risk. As soon as we get the money, we'll tell her folks that we'll drop Lorna off up the road where they can collect her."

"And when she doesn't show up? They're bound to be in touch with the other parents. What if it makes them wary of dealing with us in the future?"

Vic mulled over her suggestion and then punched his thigh. "You may have something there. Didn't you think to raise the point sooner?"

"To be fair, it's only just come to mind."

"Well, it's too late to rearrange things now, everything has been put into place, and we'll be good to go in a couple of hours." He unhooked his arm and got to his feet. "I'm going to see to the van. Keep an eye on things around here."

She held out a hand, and he latched on to it. "Stay safe."

"Safe is my middle name. I'll be back soon."

April stood at the lounge window and watched him drive off, thoughts of leaving him a distant memory now that they had a new initiative in place. If all went well, they'd be sunning themselves in Monte Carlo, sipping cocktails by the pool, with a healthy sum sitting in the bank. *Money truly is the root of all evil, and I'm relishing getting my hands on it.*

April went back upstairs to collect the plates. She listened at James's door; he was still sobbing. She decided to leave him to it, not really knowing what to say to console him. She'd done her best when she'd been in there earlier. He hadn't been prepared to listen then, so there was no point thinking now would be any different. She descended the stairs and waited for Vic to return. Feelings of trepidation emerged, and she paced the lounge until the van pulled up outside the cottage.

Not long to go now!

* * *

WHILE CLAIRE HANDED around the pizza and Suzanna poured the drinks, Sam ran through the plans for the second time that evening. "So, we're going to hit the two properties at ten, the same time as we trap the kidnappers. We've got no way of knowing how big this operation is, how many criminals are involved. It could be two or twenty for all we know. I've organised several patrols to join in the raids at both properties. We'll keep the numbers light at the drop-off location, only because we'll have the ART on hand."

"Where do you want me?" Bob asked.

"At the cottage, it's a smaller target than the farm."

"In other words, I won't be running around like a headless chicken."

"I was thinking more hobbling around, rather than running." Sam grinned.

"Whatever," he mumbled, clearly miffed by her decision to have Alex riding alongside her when it mattered, instead of him, despite her warning earlier, which he had seemed to be okay with at the time.

She stepped closer and lowered her voice. "Don't be such a grouch. It makes sense not to have you in the thick of the action, matey."

"Yeah, I know. It doesn't stop it hurting, though, does it?"

"Work on getting that cast off and back to normal, and everything will be hunky-dory again, won't it?"

"I suppose. I'm doing my best. It's ticking me off as much as it is you."

"I feel for you. You'll soon be up and running again. See what I did there?"

"Yeah, it wasn't worth a titter from me, sorry, boss."

"Whatever." Sam walked back to the desk at the front of the room.

They all tucked into their pizza and coffee as they bounced several ideas around.

IT WAS APPROXIMATELY a fifty-minute drive to Rydal from the station, but Sam allowed an hour, just to cover any unforeseen circumstances arising. The team set off in a convoy with Sam and Alex leading the way.

"How are you feeling?" she asked her stand-in partner for the evening.

"It's going to be a breeze, boss. Don't worry about me, I'll take my lead from you."

"Let's hope we can pull this off."

"In that wig, you could pull anything off." Alex laughed.

Sam angled her rear-view and studied herself. She'd never considered going blonde before. She still wasn't sure it suited her. She returned the mirror to its original position. "I hope a sudden wind doesn't pick up and wrench it off my head. Not sure how people cope, wearing one permanently, unless they're stuck on with super glue."

"It takes all sorts, I suppose."

"Unless they have a medical condition to worry about, I can't see why anyone would choose to wear one. I'm having to resist the temptation to scratch my scalp all the time."

"Hopefully, it won't be for too long."

The conversation died between them. Sam kept an eye on the satnav, her anticipation mounting as she watched the miles counting down.

They arrived at Rydal Hall with ten minutes to spare. She

breathed out a relieved sigh and scanned the area. "Glad the satnav didn't take us on a wild and unexpected adventure. I've never been here before, have you?"

"Years ago. Don't worry, I was keeping an eye on the route. I would have pointed it out if she had taken us the wrong way."

"She? Why are you being gender specific?" she asked with the straightest face she could summon.

"I… umm…"

She laughed. "I was teasing. Trying to lighten the atmosphere. I think we should check in with the others while we've got the time."

It had been a couple of miles since they had separated from the rest of the team. She rang Bob first. "Hey, how's it going at your end?"

"Can we leave my end out of this?"

"Bob Jones, do you seriously think this is the right time to be larking about?"

"Ugh… sorry. You know what I'm like."

"Only too well, unfortunately. Now answer the damn question."

"All quiet here. No lights on in the cottage, not from the front anyway."

"They could be on around the back, so don't be too eager to dismiss the idea that no one is home."

"I won't. Claire and I have it covered here."

"I'll check in with you later." She ended the call and took Alex's phone from him. "Is this Suzanna?"

"I thought I'd make myself useful for a change."

"Good man. Hi, Suzanna, are you in position?"

"We are, boss. All quiet here at the moment. We've got activity in the farmhouse."

"Do you have a good view of all the property from where you are? The barns and outbuildings for instance?"

"They're off to the right, some of them. Yes, we've got a good view. We can hear a tractor in one of the fields nearby."

"Could be on a neighbouring farm. Keep your eyes and ears open and be ready to go at ten."

"Leave it with us, boss. We'll be in touch after the raid."

"Speak later. Take care."

Sam continued to scan the area around them. There was one way into the estate, and they were parked on the edge of it. "Here we go, I can see a car approaching behind. It must be the Farrars, they're early."

"Eager to get this over with, I shouldn't wonder." Alex shifted in his seat to glance behind him. "Two vehicles, the ART are right behind them."

"Great. I was hoping to deal with the commander of the response team first. I'll stick with that, the Farrars can wait for a moment." Sam and Alex exited the vehicle. "You make the Farrars aware of the situation for me, Alex."

"On my way."

The ART vehicle squeezed past the Farrars' car and drew to a halt alongside Sam.

The commander hopped out and approached her. "Nice to see you again, sir."

"Who are these people?" Commander Endicott demanded.

"They're the parents of the girl being exchanged. I asked them to meet me here at nine-forty-five, they're early. They can wait while we run through our plan, no problem."

"I don't like the thought of them being here, but if that's okay with you... How is this going to go down then?" He frowned and asked, "You're not usually blonde, are you?"

Sam smiled. "I'm in disguise, pretending to be the mother in order to make the exchange."

"Ah, yes, good idea. And the exchange is due to take place at the church?"

"Yes, just up the road. Are you familiar with the area?"

"I know it well enough. We have the Ordinance Survey maps on board, we can find suitable viewing positions before we head over to the location. I want to be there at least twenty minutes before the allotted time."

"I agree. Is there anything else you need from me?"

He thumbed over his shoulder. "I need you to keep them out of our hair, can you do that?"

"I'm hoping so. Are we finished here?"

"I believe we are. We're going to head to the location. Will you be driving their vehicle?"

"Might be a bonus if we did. I'll have a word, see if they agree. I don't think the husband is too happy we're involved."

He shrugged. "Tough titties as my old mum used to say. If he wants his daughter back unharmed, there's no other way around this, is there?"

"That's what I told Mrs Farrar. I'll see you over there. We'll make the exchange and step back towards the car."

"That'll be our cue to finish off the operation. Good luck."

"Let's hope this all goes according to plan." She walked towards the Farrars' vehicle.

The couple were standing alongside Alex, looking anxiously at what was going on around them.

"Hi, I'm not going to ask how either of you are this evening, it's obvious. What I would like to do is reassure you that we have extensive measures in place to safeguard everyone's safety."

"An ART is present, all that is doing is striking fear into my heart, Inspector," Mr Farrar said.

Sam sighed. "It's procedure for them to be in attendance, sir. You're going to need to trust us."

"Do you seriously think we'd be here if we didn't?" he replied gruffly.

"Oscar, please. You promised me you'd keep that temper

of yours in check," Vanessa said. She placed a hand on her husband's arm, but he moved away from her.

He grunted. "I'm as calm as I need to be."

"Time is slipping away from us. Do you have the money?" Sam asked.

Mr Farrar opened the boot of his car and pointed at the black briefcase. He flipped the catch to reveal the money. "It's all there, a hundred grand that we can ill afford to lose."

"Hopefully, that won't be the case. I have a favour to ask… for authenticity purposes, would it be okay if my partner and I use your vehicle to make the exchange?"

Mr Farrar stared at her for a long moment as if working through the different options open to him. It was his wife who stepped in and answered.

"Yes, that would make perfect sense for you to go in our car, wouldn't it, Oscar?"

He nodded. "Okay, as long as you take care of it."

"That goes without saying, sir. We're going to need to say farewell to you both now." She handed Mr Farrar the keys of her car. "I'll do you a swap. You can wait in my car. We'll collect you once the operation is over."

Mr Farrar took the keys and stood back with his wife, allowing Sam and Alex to hop into their Mercedes.

"We hope all goes well," Mrs Farrar called after them.

Sam reversed and made the short trip to Rydal church. "Here we go. Are you ready for this, Alex?"

"Should we do it together? Hand over the money? Who have the kidnappers been dealing with?"

"That's a great idea. Yes, I believe they've been in contact with Mr Farrar." Sam glanced in the rear-view mirror. "I can see headlights approaching behind. Have a quick look. Can you see the armed officers anywhere?"

Between them, they quickly scoured the area.

"Nope, they must be well hidden, boss."

"Good. So we hand over the money and step back towards the vehicle, that's the cue the commander will be waiting for before he reacts."

"God, I hope this doesn't go belly up."

"It won't, not if we do everything according to plan. Think positive, man. We've got this."

The black van eased forward and drew up beside them.

"You're in charge, for now," Sam uttered out of the corner of her mouth.

"Shit! Okay, should we get out of the vehicle now or wait for them to make the first move?"

Sam viewed the time on the clock: one minute to ten. "Wait another minute, the others will be getting ready to begin their missions. We need to be in sync if this is going to work."

The kidnappers remained in their van until ten, then the male exited it, leaving his door open, and approached them.

"Let's go, it's ten now."

Alex got out of the car first, and then Sam followed.

"Where's the money?" the male demanded.

"It's in the boot. I'll get it for you. Where's my daughter?" Alex pointed at the back of the car.

"She's in the van."

"I want to see her before I hand over the money."

The kidnapper shook his head. "You might think you're in control of this situation, but you're not. Give me the money, and we'll do the exchange."

Alex lifted the boot and removed the briefcase.

"Open it. It could be full of rocks for all I know."

"It's not. It has my life's savings in here," Alex replied, surprising Sam.

She clung to his arm and said in a shaky voice, acting her part well, "Open it, dear. If it means us getting our daughter back."

"You should listen to your wife, she talks a lot of sense, for a *woman*." The kidnapper laughed.

The door of the van opened, and the woman got out and stood beside the male.

Alex flipped the catch, and the briefcase opened to reveal the bundles of twenties.

The male reached out a hand to touch the notes, but Alex wrenched the case away. "My daughter first."

The male stared at him for a few stress-filled moments and then removed a large knife from his sleeve. "You're in no position to argue the toss with me. You're the one putting your daughter's life at risk, not me."

"Please, Oscar, just give him the money. I want Lorna back unharmed."

Reluctantly, Alex handed over the case. The male took it and ran his hands over the cash. He then closed the case and handed it to the woman. "Put it in the van."

She rushed back to the van and hopped in the front.

"Where's our daughter?" Alex demanded.

The male waved the knife towards him. "We'll release her up the road."

"What? No way. We won't allow you to take her with you," Alex shouted.

Sam latched on to his arm. "Darling, we don't have an option. Stay calm."

The man waved the knife at Alex. "Shut the fuck up. I'm in charge, not you. You do what I say, not the other way around."

Sam's phone vibrated in her pocket. She ground her teeth, anxious to read the message one of her team had obviously sent her. "Please, Oscar, listen to him." Then, turning to the kidnapper, she said, "There's no need for anyone to get hurt. You have the money, all we want is our daughter returned to us, unharmed."

"And I've already told you, we're going to drive away and drop her in a lay-by up the road. Now stand back."

Sam and Alex took a few paces backwards, and shouts rang out all around them.

"Armed police, drop your weapon."

"A set-up? Really? Consider your daughter dead."

He thrust forward and attempted to stab Alex in the chest, but Sam used several karate chops in quick succession to force him to drop the weapon. Then the man panicked and ran towards the van. Shots rang out.

"No, don't shoot," Sam shouted. "We haven't got the girl yet."

The male took a bullet in the leg. He staggered towards the van. Another shot hit his other leg, immobilising him completely.

The woman flew out of the van and ran to her fellow kidnapper. "Vic, are you hurt?"

Sam and Alex made their move as the armed police marched forward, their guns still aimed at the two suspects. Sam and Alex slapped the cuffs on the suspects, then Sam searched the back of the van. Lorna was nowhere to be seen.

She returned to the suspects, grabbed the man by the hair and shouted, "Where is she?"

The man let out a hysterical laugh, and the woman sobbed.

"She's dead," the woman whispered.

Sam pulled the woman's arm, forcing her to her feet. "What are you talking about?"

"Keep your mouth shut," Vic shouted.

The woman shook her head as the tears tumbled down her cheeks. "She died. She was a diabetic. We tried to help... but... she didn't make it."

"So you thought you'd get the money out of her parents, adding to their misery. You're scum, no worse than that."

The commander arrived. "What's going on? Where's the hostage?"

"Apparently, there isn't one. She's already dead. Can you deal with these two? I need to contact my teams, see what they've uncovered."

"Leave them with me." The commander instructed two of his men to take the suspects to their vehicle.

Sam withdrew her phone from her pocket and checked her messages. There was one from Bob.

HOSTAGES all at the first location. We've got them... all except Lorna. Her boyfriend is in a right state. He's not making any sense. He said she's dead.

WHICH CONFIRMED what the kidnappers had told her. "Shit! How am I going to tell her parents?"

"Do you want me to do it, boss?" Alex asked, chivalrously.

"No. I'll do it. I've heard from Bob, the other hostages are safe."

"That's great news. So where's the girl's body?"

Sam sighed. "That's what we need to find out. Jesus, I hoped it wasn't going to end like this. Come on, we'd better drive back and break the news to Lorna's parents."

"Jesus, that's not going to go down well, is it? Do you want me to drive?"

Sam nodded. "If you wouldn't mind."

They hopped back into the Farrars' Merc, and Alex reversed into the clearing and drove out onto the main road. The Farrars glanced up when they heard them approaching. They both rushed forward and peered in the back seat of their car.

"Where is she?" Sam heard Mr Farrar ask through her partially open window.

Sam and Alex got out.

Sam had the wig in her hand. She ran a hand through her hair to fluff it up. "You'll be pleased to know we have the kidnappers in custody."

"That's not what I asked. Where is Lorna?" Mr Farrar's eyes flared with rage.

"Oscar, don't shout. Let her speak."

"I'm sorry. They told us your daughter had died. A member of my team has confirmed their claim is true."

Mrs Farrar dropped to her knees and howled. Mr Farrar looked a broken man. He stared down at his wife, apparently unable to move.

Sam knelt beside Mrs Farrar and held her in her arms. "I'm so sorry. I think she was already dead. It had nothing to do with what went on this evening."

"It doesn't matter. My baby is gone. I'll never hold her in my arms again. This can't be happening."

"I want those people to suffer as much as we're suffering. How dare they extort this money out of us, knowing that she was already dead?" Mr Farrar said through gritted teeth.

"I believe she died from complications due to her diabetes," Sam replied, trying her best to justify their daughter's death, rightly or wrongly.

"If she wasn't put under the stress of being kidnapped, she would have survived and received the medical attention she required. They killed her, nothing you can say to the contrary will make me think otherwise," Mr Farrar stated authoritatively.

"Obviously, that will all be taken into consideration once the case gets to court, sir. You have my condolences. We did our very best for it not to end this way."

"Did you? I'll be issuing a formal complaint. This investigation has been flawed from the word go."

Mrs Farrar got to her feet and flew at her husband, beating at his chest with her fists. "Oscar, don't say that. You're the one who warned me not to get in touch with the inspector. If I had listened to your wishes, the kidnappers would have succeeded in getting away with the money tonight. Don't be such a downright bastard."

Mr Farrar stood there, shocked at his wife's hostility. He clearly didn't know how to respond and sought Sam's help.

She stepped forward and gently cradled his sobbing wife. "Please don't do this. This is no one's fault but the kidnappers'. We'll get Lorna the justice she deserves, I promise."

Mr Farrar tapped Sam on the shoulder. "I think my wife and I need to be alone now, Inspector."

Sam nodded, and she and Alex got back in Sam's car. She sat behind the steering wheel for a few moments, collecting her thoughts, and then started the engine. "We need to put this behind us and build a solid case that will send these bastards down for life."

"I couldn't agree more, boss. Are you okay to drive?"

"I'm fine. Let's see what's going on at the cottage."

Bob greeted them with a strained smile.

"Everything all right, Bob?" Sam asked.

"Not really. James is devastated. He tried to get the kidnappers to help Lorna. They refused to seek medical help. She fell into a coma, and her body began to shut down. He was tied up, there was nothing he could have done to assist her."

"That's going to live with him for the rest of his life, poor man. What about the other hostages, are they all fit and well?"

"Yes, they appear to be. I've called for an ambulance. There's going to be a slight delay in the crew getting here."

"Don't worry, we're not in a rush to leave, are we?"

Bob shook his head. "Nope. What about the parents, have you broken the news to them?"

"Yes. It was difficult, for all of us. The father accused me of letting them down or not having my pulse on the investigation."

"Ignore him. He's lashing out, looking for someone to blame."

"That's going to be hard, when he files a complaint against me."

"Shit! Did he say that?"

"Yep. I'm done with this. All right if I leave you here? I want to get back to the station to interview the suspects."

"Why don't you go home instead? That can wait until tomorrow."

"No, it can't. I want it over and done with tonight."

"Alex, you go with the boss. I'll take care of things here."

"Let me know when you're on your way back," Sam said. "Thanks, Bob."

SAM HAD SPENT the last ten minutes ringing around the rest of the families involved, letting them know that their children were safe. Now she had the onerous task of interviewing the female suspect. The duty solicitor was already present. The time was ten past twelve in the morning. April sat opposite, her head down and her hands clasped firmly together.

"Where's Vic?" she asked.

"On his way to the hospital. I'll question him in the morning. What was the motive behind the kidnappings, April?"

April's focus remained on the desk, and she refused to answer.

"If you want the judge to treat you favourably, it would be wise for you to open up to me. The motive behind you kidnapping the three couples was?"

April inhaled a large breath. "People trafficking. We had a contact lined up. You scuppered the deal, plastering our faces over the TV."

"I see. So you had to change your plans at the last minute and came up with the idea of asking for the ransom?"

"That's right. We were out of pocket and needed to recoup our losses."

"When did Lorna die?"

April shifted in her chair. "I'm not sure. I just found her."

"And where is her body?"

"We buried her in the back garden."

"You both had a hand in burying her?"

She nodded.

"Can you confirm it for the recording?"

"Yes, we both dug her grave."

"Did you try to help her before she died?"

"Yes, you have to believe me."

"Only James, her boyfriend, is telling us a different story. He said he tried to ask for medical assistance as she'd slipped into a coma, and you refused to ring for help. Is that true?"

April swallowed and ran a hand over her face. "I tried. Vic was the one digging his heels in."

"What use would she have been to you dead?"

"She wouldn't have been."

"So why didn't you impress that upon Vic?" Sam studied the bruises, varying in colour, around her eyes and covering both cheeks.

"Did he beat you?"

April sat there, not saying a word.

"Where did the bruises come from? I'm not blind, April. Did you carry out his plans willingly or under duress?"

The solicitor leaned towards April and whispered something in her ear. Sam closed her eyes, knowing what was about to come out of April's mouth next.

"No comment."

"Is that how the rest of this interview is going to go?"

April grinned and said, "No comment."

"Okay, it's late. I'll stop the interview now and question you again tomorrow. It'll give you time to contemplate the trouble you're in, and it might even prompt you into making the right decision in the morning, when we meet up again. Sleep well, Miss Wilson."

"I will," she replied smugly.

Sam and Alex left the constable, who had also been present in the room, to return April to her cell and went back upstairs to the incident room. The rest of the team looked shattered and were sitting around, drinking coffee.

"Great, you're back. How did it go?" Sam asked.

"Only been back five minutes or so," Bob replied. "The paramedics checked everyone over and gave them the all clear. We dropped the hostages back to their families before we returned to base."

"That's great news. I've interviewed the female," Sam said. "She told me this was all to do with people trafficking but the deal turned sour thanks to me putting their faces out there."

Bob nodded. "Well done, boss. I had my doubts whether you were doing the right thing or not, mentioning the van and showing their images during the conference."

"That'll teach you to doubt me next time, won't it? Okay, it's gone one now, let's go home and start over again in the morning. Don't bother coming in until ten, that's an order."

The team drifted off, and Sam took the lift with Bob.

"We did good, eh?" she said. "Even though you were hampered by your bum leg."

"I'll have you know, I worked through the discomfort on this one, boss."

"I don't doubt it." She patted him on the back as the lift doors squeaked open.

Sam was surprised to find Nick still on duty. "I thought you'd left hours ago. How's your wife?"

"I nipped home for a few hours but said I'd fill in to make up the time, ma'am. Umm… she's fine. The doctor has put her on HRT to try and sort her out."

"Really, to cure her headaches?"

"A combination of different ailments. She's been a pain in the arse to live with the past few months."

"Ah, right. Well, let's hope both your lives will be better once the meds kick in. See you in the morning."

"Another investigation successfully put to bed."

"Thankfully."

Sam helped Bob into his vehicle and drove home.

EPILOGUE

*S*am crept into the house and found Rhys sitting in the lounge, waiting for her, Sonny on one side of him on the sofa and Benji on the other.

"Yikes, caught in the act. I know you don't allow them on the furniture."

She laughed. "Extenuating circumstances acceptable. Did I wake you?"

"I was dozing. Glad to see you home safely. Can I get you a drink or something to eat?"

"No. All I want to do is fall into bed." She glanced at the coffee table in front of him. The letter she'd received was poking out of the envelope. Her gaze drifted up to his face again. "You read it?" It was a genuine question, not an accusation.

"Sorry, kick me out now if I've overstepped the mark."

"Sonny, can you move over?"

Sonny lazily shifted to the end of the sofa, and she sat next to Rhys.

He gathered her hands in his. "Why didn't you tell me? How long have you had it?"

"A few days. In all honesty, the investigation took over, and I put it on hold. What do you think?"

"I'd better not reveal what I truly think of your ex. How can he do this to you?"

She shrugged. "I suppose it was to be expected. We bought the house together, and he did most of the renovations on it."

"He also landed you with a lot of debt. What are you going to do about it?"

"I'll have to sell up. Although Crystal has told me I can borrow some money from her pension pot and pay it back in instalments."

He held her gaze for a few minutes and then said, "Or I could move in and take over some of the bills, maybe stump up some cash up front, enough for you to pay Chris off."

Sam gasped. "I can't ask you to do that."

"You didn't. I offered. It's late now, let's discuss it over dinner tomorrow, instead."

"Blimey, drop a bombshell like that and end the conversation in the same breath. Go you."

He grinned and touched her face. "You've had a long day. You probably won't be thinking straight. We'll discuss it when you're in a better frame of mind."

She shook her head. "I don't have to think about it." She leaned forward and kissed him. "This feels right, you and me. Do you really think we can make a go of it, together?"

"I'm willing to give it a try if you are."

"On one proviso."

He cocked his head and queried, "What's that?"

"That you adhere to my rules..."

"Rules?"

"No dogs on the sofa."

He laughed and placed his hands on either side of her face, sucking her into a kiss that took her breath away.

THE END

THANK you for reading another adventure in the DI Sam Cobbs series, book 6 **To Punish Them** is now available.

MAYBE YOU'D ALSO LIKE to try one of my other edge-of-your-seat thriller series. Grab the first book in the bestselling, award-winning Justice series here, <u>Cruel Justice.</u>

OR THE FIRST book in the spin-off Justice Again series, <u>Gone In Seconds.</u>

OR MY OTHER super successful police procedural series set in Hereford. Find the first book in the DI Sara Ramsey series, <u>No Right to Kill</u>

PERHAPS YOU'D PREFER to try one of my other police procedural series, the DI Kayli Bright series which begins with <u>The Missing Children.</u>

OR MAYBE YOU'D enjoy the DI Sally Parker series set in Norfolk, <u>Wrong Place.</u>

OR MY GRITTY police procedural starring DI Nelson set in Manchester, <u>Torn Apart.</u>

. . .

OR MY BEST-SELLING psychological thriller She's Gone.

KEEP IN TOUCH WITH M A COMLEY HERE...

Pick up a FREE novella by signing up to my newsletter today.
https://BookHip.com/WBRTGW

BookBub
www.bookbub.com/authors/m-a-comley

Blog

http://melcomley.blogspot.com

Why not join my special Facebook group to take part in monthly giveaways.

Readers' Group

Made in the USA
Las Vegas, NV
24 July 2022

52112254R10125